To the

Best Wishes

MORGWEL
HALL

Michael Hutchins

20.09.19

First published 2018

Published under licence by Brown Dog Books and The Self-Publishing Partnership, 7 Green Park Station, Bath BA1 1JB

www.selfpublishingpartnership.co.uk

ISBN printed book: 978-1-78545-373-1
ISBN e-book: 978-1-78545-374-8

Cover design by Kevin Rylands
Internal design by Andrew Easton

Printed and bound by CPI Group (UK) Ltd, Croydon, CR0 4YY

MORGWEL HALL

MICHAEL HUTCHINS

BROWN DOG BOOKS

CHAPTER 1

1921

The House

The first time I saw Morgwel Hall I fell instantly in love: the long, curving, tree-lined drive of copper beech trees, the perfectly formed, immaculate hedgerows, the babbling brook dancing along the borders... Had I at last indeed found my heaven?

You see, I fall in love easily and it was to happen twice that day, though the second instance was a mystery, one that was to stretch my mind to its utmost limit – and to this day still does.

My name is Andrew Williamson, Captain, that is, though I have just been released, or given the all-clear as I prefer, after three long years in recovery. You see, I am a victim, or survivor, depending on your outlook, of what was to become known as The Great War.

'So here we have it, sir.'

'What?' I replied, my mind, as so often, drifting from the present reality back, back to the depths of my former despair.

The enthusiastic estate agent had stopped our vehicle for the 'vista', as he described it, of Morgwel Hall.

I raised my eyes and gulped in a breath of air: yes, this was truly my idea of Heaven. My trusty Border collie Brigadier Hague (my personal joke) was making his strange snuffling noise when he wanted to go outside. I opened the door and he leaped to the floor, setting off immediately to explore this strange and unfamiliar place.

Following my long, arduous journey to better health in a Scottish recovery hospital, or for me just trying to live a normal life, I had often dreamed – yes, longed – for the wild, open expanse of Cornwall. The dramatic cliffs, never-ending beaches, the brilliant blue skies: the peace, yes, the peace was my dream.

'Sir, are you feeling all right? A glass of water maybe?'

The black patch covering my left eye had differing effects on those around me: to some it was a romantic, dashing trophy of war; to others it was a sign of pain, maybe a weakness and an anomaly as to how they should treat me, as was my profound limp.

'What? Oh sorry, Mr James. Yes, golly, what a lovely picture – almost too good to paint.'

Can I do it justice? I pondered. Can I make this scene come alive? My portraits of Passchendaele were to become legendary, but for now I wanted to put that period of my life in a box and throw away the key.

In the distance I could hear the crashing and pounding of waves as the relentless sea battered the shoreline. It was high tide and the wonderful sounds felt as though they were sitting next to me, a far cry from the incessant thud of artillery.

'No water, Mr James, thank you. Oh and please I should like to walk the remaining distance to the house if you please.'

'Why of course, sir.'

The man was irritating me as he jumped from the automobile and opened my door, his enthusiasm to sell far too apparent. I needed to fall in love. I didn't care how many rooms there were, how much land, or about the servants' quarters. I needed to be alone.

I took my polished elm walking cane and steadied myself as a sudden gust of wind blew across the beaten clifftop, hitting me with its gentle force. I stood still and silent, taking a deep breath of the sea air. Yes, this was Heaven.

'So shall I see you up at the house, sir?'

'What? Oh yes don't mind this.' I waved my walking stick. 'I am quite mobile. I need to take in the atmosphere.'

'Of course, sir, whatever you wish.'

The irritating little man climbed back into the vehicle, crashing the gears as he engaged them and pushing the accelerator far too hard, causing the engine to rev high. A plume of brilliant blue smoke escaped from the exhaust. Then I was alone as he navigated the long drive.

My eyes traversed the stunning countryside down to the cliff edges, then to the never-ending expanse of brilliant blue sea, but I could feel a sweat coming on, a panic. I fumbled for my saviour, then I found it: the silver hip flask.

I gulped greedily at the malt whisky as the liquid hit my throat: the wonderful warm feeling as it journeyed to my stomach, then calm, peace. I was again at one with my surroundings.

I looked at the battered Victorian object, a present for my 21st, it was solid silver with numerous dents and one large one, a reminder of the German bullet that had ricocheted off into the sandbags of my trench.

Yes, this was my saviour in many ways.

My leg was particularly painful that day. Though the gout had not returned for many months, the wound from a piece of shrapnel had opened again, with droplets of blood staining the brilliant white bandage and causing a small patch on my trouser leg.

Then my twisted mind began to journey back to the memory of Elizabeth, my Lizzie, the most wonderful, beautiful woman who had walked on this planet: her flowing locks, that tiny waist, her fragile frame... God, how I missed her.

This was yet another burden to carry in my short, young life. Lizzie, the love of my life, had died in 1919 from the Spanish influenza. She had moved to Scotland to be near me but, like many millions, had succumbed to the Black Death of the 20th century.

I steadied myself then began to walk the gentle incline to the house. The copper beech ended, giving way to a circular parking area, the ornate fountain centrepiece trickling with water. I imagined the horse-drawn carriages of a grand yesteryear pulling up, their wealthy passengers attending a ball, dinner or luncheon.

To the right was a castellated round tower, perhaps a relic of a former castle, and then from the corner of my eye I spotted HER for the first time high up in the half-ruined stones. My dog

Dougy was kicking up a fuss, barking and running frantically around the base.

The sun made my focus difficult but as my eyes adjusted, yes, there she was, a stunning apparition: a young girl in a grey shawl dancing carefree, spinning round, laughing. I rubbed my eyes, looking back at the building, but she had disappeared.

The short, tough walk had sapped my strength as I stood still gaping at the sheer beauty of the place.

'Brigadier, here, boy. Come, stop that barking.' (His full name was Brigadier Douglas Hague: he had recall to both 'Dougy' and 'Brigadier.') He ran enthusiastically to my side, his deep brown eyes looking adoringly at me, waiting for a command.

'Good boy, come, wait,' I ordered then, pausing, my eyes were briefly drawn back towards the ruins but they were alas empty.

'Mr James, sir, if you please, but who was that I saw in the old castle?'

He looked back directly at me, nervous, almost defensive.

'Oh what, sir? Sorry, nothing. The house is empty and has been for a couple of years.' He coughed a strange, false cough almost as though forcing it.

'So anyhow, sir, what do you think? Is it not just the most wonderful place in the whole world?'

As much as the little creep irritated me I had to agree it was pure joy, but why had it not been sold, nay snapped up, in a jiffy? It worried me, but then I turned and the silence, the solitude, had me hooked.

James fiddled with the huge collection of keys but finally opened the massive oak front door, its ancient timbers creaking in anger, almost objecting to being forced to move after so many years of little use.

'I am sorry, Mr James, but I am certain there was a young lady in the tower. She had a grey shawl, flowing hair and was dancing in circles.'

'Sorry, sir, really I am the only one with keys and the castle can only be accessed from the main house.' He hesitated, still sounding unconvincing. 'It was probably a shadow or the sun: I am sure there is an innocent explanation. Come, let me show you around.'

Innocent explanation: that was a strange thing to say, I pondered. What is it he is trying to hide?

'So, Mr James, please, before we enter, a little history. Morgwel Hall: that's an interesting name, please tell me more.'

'Yes, sir, of course. I can tell you are not from these parts,' came the smug reply. 'Well, see, originally it was called Kastel Hall, that's Cornish for castle, but well, the owners in Victorian times wanted a more grand name to befit their standing in the community so they renamed it Sea View Hall or Morgwel. If you ask me it's grander to have a house called a castle, but I think "Morgwel" probably flows better off the tongue, so to speak.'

He gestured me to enter the large hallway. Treading wearily into the old building I was pleasantly surprised: instead of darkness it was lit by several lamps which were glowing in the gloom, lighting the otherwise dull room. I raised an eyebrow as if to say 'how?'

'Oh sorry, sir, I should have explained. I got the petrol generator going while you were walking up the drive. Previous owners were a very wealthy family, didn't spare a penny, so you have all the modern conveniences,' beamed the once again overzealous agent. 'Oh I should also infrm you it is one of the few houses in the area connected to the National Grid which of course can easily be reinstated by the new owners.'

Dougy scampered through my legs, eager to explore the inside of the house, and soon disappearing from sight, his overgrown toenails scraping along the stone floor.

'Sir, after you,' beckoned the agent.

Once inside he fumbled with his papers. 'Now then, Captain, sir, I am sure you have the full specs, but would you like me just to go over the inventory with you?'

'Please, Mr James. Just one thing: it appears to be furnished?'

'Yes, well, not every room: owner's not bothered. It comes with the house, so to speak: if you buy the property it's yours to do whatever you so wish.'

'Mr James, sorry to be so bold but I really would like to be left alone, just to wander round by myself. Is that possible please?'

'Well, sir, highly irregular: you see, I am not supposed to let anyone alone.'

I flashed two crisp one-pound notes before the timid man. 'I noticed a nice pub back in the village: why don't I treat you? Have a bite to eat, nice pint, eh, just for an hour or so?'

'Well, sir, don't really know. I suppose it will be all right, just between me and you, like?'

'Of course, man, mum's the word. I am an officer and a gentleman.'

I offered the money which he grabbed eagerly, comically glancing around the deserted room as if checking no one had seen the transaction. He turned quickly, making for the door, then he was gone.

Examining my hunter I noted the time, and then placed it carefully back into my waistcoat. I selected a worn leather hall chair, together with another beside an open fireplace, and made myself comfortable. Pulling the house details from a brown envelope, I settled down to read before viewing the property. Dougy, now seemingly bored or having explored enough, lay at my feet.

A magnificent opportunity, a once-in-a-lifetime purchase. A ten-bedroom house with nursery, far-reaching views, suitable for a family or a discerning gentleman, plus castle ruins. 20 acres, private pathway to the beach.

The main residence includes an entrance hall, basement, kitchen scullery, wine room, library, smokers' room, living room, sewing room, snug, second living room, and link to castle ruins.

'Goodness, Dougy old man, are we going to rattle around in this or what?'

But already I had formed an attachment, a bond, though it must sound ridiculous to feel such a way about bricks and mortar. But slowly I was being sucked into the charm and mystery of Morgwel.

I decided to explore the upstairs, first climbing the main staircase; there was a second back one for servants. I felt at peace: the house for me had an air that I can't explain; though there was a sadness, I felt there had also been many happy times. I made a mental note to quiz James more about the history.

There was a long main corridor leading to the smaller corridors into the wings of the house. As I ventured slowly I noticed that each bedroom door was open. I peered into the first that was obviously the master with an adjoining bathroom and stunning sea views.

'Mm, that do you and me, eh, old man?' Dougy wagged his tail as if in agreement. 'Mm that's nice also.' Then I reached the 'T' junction turning; to the left there was a closed door. Dougy began to growl and backed away.

'Come on, you daft dog, what's up?'

Then from the room I heard a noise, a strange whimper almost like a child crying. 'Hello, who's there please?' Silence: no reply. 'I say, please make yourself known.' I heard what appeared to be footsteps, then a bang as if a door had been shut. Dougy had disappeared along the hallway.

I reached for the handle, gently opening the door and fumbled for the light switch: it was the old nursery, everything in place as if the occupants had left in a hurry. Then I heard the bang again, noting it was only a window shutter hitting the wall. I secured it firmly with the brass lock.

'Mm, see? Daft. Amazing what your mind can do,' I mumbled to myself but then shivered: the room had a damp, musty feel and the atmosphere was quite uninviting and foreboding. I peered carefully across the gloom.

A magnificent doll's house was perched in the corner with various other toys, two brass bedsteads, then, taking pride of place, a magnificent wooden rocking horse. I rubbed my eyes: it appeared to be moving, then on closer examination it appeared still, though the dust surrounding it had definitely been disturbed.

I shivered once more; I could feel a strange presence as though there was someone else in the room. It was eerie the way the toys were almost standing to attention, waiting to be played with. I decided to exit and explore the downstairs. I closed the door, heading for the back staircase.

As I reached the hall I could hear sobbing from the kitchen. Dougy was frantic, barking, sniffing at the door. I again called out, 'Hello, who is it please? Who is there?' Then there was silence. I gingerly pushed the door open, peering carefully inside and slightly holding back, afraid there was maybe someone illicit in the house with me, but no, the room was empty.

Dougy had once more calmed down, probably bored with the new game, and was lying in an old wicker dog basket adjacent to the range. I peered through the gloom, but, just like the nursery, as expected, it was quite empty. Again I sensed a strange atmosphere, as though someone or indeed something had been there.

I continued my exploration with relish, falling deeper and deeper under the spell of the house. On entering the library I marvelled at row after row of books: there must be thousands, I considered. Could they really be leaving these, too? I speculated.

I moved to the smokers' room, the grand open fireplace dominating the space with bottles of port and smoking paraphernalia dotted around the furniture, but I still could not find the entrance to the castle.

I entered the second sitting room that I knew was near to it, finally spotting a huge, old oak door with iron staples and hinges, but sadly it was locked.

'Damn it,' I mumbled to myself. 'Damn and blast.' I foraged around, looking for a key but alas, to no avail, coming to the conclusion that Mr James must have it. To the right were double doors leading to the garden. I pushed the security bolts and opened them.

A sudden gust of fresh air hit my face, making me realise just how stale the inside of Morgwel Hall had become, but I knew I was completely hooked and would make an offer today.

As I sauntered through the grounds, about 100 yards from the property I turned and once more gazed at the castle, the fine Norman keep rising majestically, silhouetted against the brilliant sun. I shaded my eyes.

Then again I saw her. I knew I was not going mad. Yes, definitely the most beautiful apparition: a girl, about my Lizzie's age, dancing and skipping, her locks flowing in the wind, the grey shawl covering her slight body.

'Hey, you, please don't go. Who are you? How did you get into the castle?' I blinked but the ruins were empty. 'What on earth?' I mumbled to myself.

I stood gaping almost breathless for minutes, time disappearing into oblivion, rubbing my eyes and looking towards the ocean, then back to the castle ruins, but sadly I was quite alone.

Resolutely I began to make my way back to the hall; re-entering the second sitting room I paused, selected a comfortable-looking, well-worn leather chair, and fell into its cavernous luxury, staring at the locked door to the castle.

Fumbling for my hip flask I lit a Player's, tugging deeply at the smoke filling my lungs with the addictive grey mist before gulping eagerly at the whisky. I stared at the door, my mind racing, then from nowhere I was back at the front line.

My men were lined in order, pushing their bodies to the walls of the trench, bayonets fixed, each one with their private fears. I checked my revolver, the whistle dangling from my neck. The rain had not stopped for days: the mud stretched as far as you could see.

My watch had misted in the damp, my clothes soaked through.

'Sir, they won't send us in this, will they?' came the voice of a young private barely out of his nappies.

'Don't worry, man,' I replied, 'The brass know what they are doing. It will be fine, just keep going once I blow my whistle,' I tried desperately to reassure the scared boy.

'Sir, don't worry, I won't let you down.'

Then along the line whistles blew and men cheered as they climbed from the trenches. I took one last look at my comrades before also blowing my whistle. We scrambled together, rising from the pit like a phoenix: then the destruction hit me.

Twisted, tormented remnants of trees reaching for the heavens dotted the otherwise lunar landscape, mud, ditches, pools of water stretching towards the enemy as men struggled to make their way forward.

All around clods of earth were dancing as thousands of machine-gun rounds hit home, then deafening explosions, mounds of earth reaching skyward as artillery rounds dropped, men screaming in the murky water, sucked under as they drowned.

This was Passchendaele, the third bloody battle of Ypres.

'Come on, men!' I screamed. 'For God, King and Country!' I scrambled from the relative safety of our trench, willing the men on, then darkness, a searing pain as the bullet hit home and I collapsed just yards into the attack.

'Sir, sir, are you all right?'

I was suddenly brought back to reality: it was Mr James the estate agent returning from his lunch, now smelling strongly of booze.

'Oh what? Yes, sorry, was just dozing off,' I lied. 'Now James, old boy, I know you keep telling me, but I can assure you I am not mad. I have definitely seen someone, a young girl carefree dancing on the battlements. Please don't belittle my intelligence. Who is she?'

'Anyhow, Captain, how was your tour?' he beamed, hastily changing the subject.

'What? Oh yes. Only thing, couldn't find the key to the castle ruins. I really do want to give it the once-over, then I will make my decision.'

CHAPTER 2

The Castle Ruins

'Why of course, follow me: it's hidden just over there.' He pointed to some crumbling brickwork. Striding across the room, he pushed one end, forcing the other to pop out, revealing a secret compartment that contained an ancient, huge, wrought-iron key covered in rust.

He placed the key in the lock which turned surprisingly easily, then tugged at the huge door which creaked slowly open into the room. 'Now then, sir, please be careful: the stairs are very steep and curve at quite an angle. I shall lead the way.'

'Actually no, Mr James, please. I wish to explore this alone.'

'Fine, sir, no problem. Just please be careful as you know I should really accompany you.'

I crossed the threshold and felt immediately I had travelled back in time: this was the lower floor with no arrowslits – in fact, total darkness.

'Sorry, Captain, sir, there is an oil lamp just inside on the ledge.'

I fumbled with my matches then suddenly the whole vista became lit: it was damp, cold, musty, a mass of cobwebs with the solid stone walls still standing strong. I moved forward, noting there were stairs to which I guessed was a basement. To one side were the remnants of a well and the other stairs leading upwards.

Holding the lamp higher I noted that the room was completely empty and surmised it had probably been the living quarters, more than likely a combined kitchen and sleeping accommodation, shared with livestock etc., as was the custom of the day.

My mind drifted to the past as the atmosphere totally engulfed me: were there any notable sieges? If so, who and how long? Why the transformation from castle to an adjacent manor house? I was completely captivated.

I decided, against my better judgement, to firstly explore the basement. There was no door, just a simple leather strap across the entrance. I held the lamp forward and peered down: a single-width, curving stone stairway disappeared into the void.

I cautiously took the first few steps, descending quite quickly: the deeper I ventured, the damper the atmosphere, the walls now slimy with dripping water. Then suddenly I was on level ground, a solid stone floor. I paused, holding the lamp, and circled slowly: it was smaller than the upstairs room and quite cold.

As I was about halfway around I stopped dead: in a corner were some ancient-looking barrels quite out of place. I stepped gingerly over to them, halting and shining my lamp; they appeared to be stacked randomly, but on closer inspection I could see they were there to hide something.

Now completely intrigued, I placed the lamp carefully on

a stone shelf and began to move the barrels; they were empty, so this was a relatively easy task. One by one I rolled them across the room until I uncovered what appeared to be a large entranceway.

This, however, had been hastily boarded up and I could quite easily see there was a tunnel or passageway. As I strained to uncover the mystery I heard a crashing noise coming from the depths below. I stopped dead, moving hastily back.

Becoming braver, I once more peered into the murky cavern. Yes, again a crashing noise now accompanied by a strange howling. I shivered. What on earth? My exhaling breath was like wisps of smoke in the still air.

The howling was almost like a human scream and menacingly frightening. I found myself quite scared as the ghostly noise seemed to reach a crescendo, then again the crashing, but as I listened I realised it appeared to be at regular intervals.

But what of the strange howling, almost human-like cries? I called out, 'Hello, who is there!?' As before there was no reply but on this occasion, instead of the noise abating, the crashing and howling continued.

Then suddenly I was hit by a gust of cold air sending shivers down my spine. Almost losing my balance, I stumbled backwards, deciding the mystery of the tunnel was for another day and turning towards the stairs.

One by one I clambered up the steep flight, now puffing hard and not quite realising on the descent just how steep they were, and behind still the incessant howling and crashing. I hurried the best I could to escape, then as the steps curved away, the sounds disappeared into oblivion, leaving once more an eerie silence.

On reaching the ground floor I realised, despite the cold and damp, I had broken into a slight but obvious sweat. Damping myself with a hanky, I took a couple of minutes to compose myself, mumbling that I needed to pull myself together.

'Right, that's below done,' I mumbled, 'now I need to explore the upstairs, see the battlements and how many other floors there are,' the excitement of the exploration returning as the adventure in the basement became just a frightening memory.

Taking a deep breath I began the climb, the stairs not quite as steep but still calling on my stamina as on the basement steps. Despite my limp and stick I managed to make good progress, the good width of the steps aiding me. I stopped on a half-landing to get my breath.

We were still too low for any significant arrowslits, but as I turned the next bend I came upon another room, the timber floorboards made of oak. There were several narrow slits for firing: I guessed I was now over 20 feet high.

Thin beams of light filtered through the firing holes, causing the disturbed dust to dance like puppets at a beach show, each one differing but appearing as strange, mystical figure-like apparitions.

More steps, my breath now quite laboured, my leg hurting, and my patched eye becoming uncomfortable as the dried sweat formed a hardened, sticky mass.

Then another timber-floored room, again empty but with more arrowslits. I was almost at the top and could see shafts of light tumbling down the staircase from the open-topped castellated tower roof.

One more short flight then fresh air as I entered the battlements. I stopped to scan the scene: some of the castellations had crumbled and thorns had invaded one corner, making their presence quite forthright.

I walked to the seaward side and gasped at the view: far below, the sea smashed its way relentlessly onto the rocks. As the tide began to ebb a small sandy cove became evident. Sea gulls danced and darted, hunting for supper. Out at sea a lone fisherman laboured for that day's catch.

A sudden gust of wind hit my face, the glorious sea air waking my senses. Yes, I had found my own private heaven. Then I turned towards the thorn bush: what was that flapping on one side?

I approached cautiously. 'No,' I gasped, 'no, it can't be,' but there in plain sight was a tangled, single thread of grey wool dancing and flowing in the wind. I walked forward and grabbed it as if my life depended on it. Pulling the thin strand to my heart, I mumbled, 'See, I know what I saw.'

I lingered, my eyes shut tightly, imagining the girl I had seen dancing on the tower, though outside there was an eerie silence. Even the cool, gentle breeze appeared to have disappeared, then without warning I heard a noise from the stairwell.

I turned, facing the entrance as the strange scratching noise grew louder and closer. My imagination was running wild: what could it be? What was I to face? Was it the girl?

Then Dougy appeared, his huge, beaming eyes sending

waves of love as he spotted me, the tail swirling and swishing like the sails of a windmill. I laughed to myself at the same time breathing a sigh of relief:, the sound no more than his claws on the stonework.

'Here, boy, come over, you scared me half to death.'

My four-legged companion trotted towards me, obviously again up for more exploration. I leaned forward, stroking his wet muzzle before ruffling his neck. Then he walked off to one side of the tower sniffing, delving and investigating as only dogs can.

'Had enough of that comfy basket, eh, old friend?'

Suddenly he stopped in front of the brambles, his fur raised, a soft growling tone emitted as he bared his teeth. Slowly he backed away, becoming fiercer by the moment.

'What's up, boy?' I enquired, turning to face him, concerned at his out of character outburst. As I did so from my peripheral vision I could swear there was the lowly figure of my mysterious girl leaning over the battlements.

But, as before, in a flash there was nobody but myself and Dougy, who was still staring towards the brambles. 'What on earth is going on, boy?'

But he was oblivious to me. Still focused on that part of the tower, he began to bark as the bush appeared to move violently. A chilling mystery: there was no wind. Then I thought I heard a scream. Venturing to the battlements, I again called out, but as before no reply, just silence.

I shivered. By now close to my dog, I gave him some comforting words and a gentle stroke which had the desired effect, as he once more become my faithful Dougy.

'Come on, old man, let's find that blooming agent and this time I want some answers.'

As we moved towards the entrance I had an uncomfortable feeling that I was being stared at, that there were eyes on me, sending shivers down my spine. Dougy was already navigating the stairs but as I reached the entrance something made me halt. I felt I was definitely not alone.

Taking a deep breath, I turned quickly – but no, just me. Then my eyes were inexplicably pulled to the wall's edge, focusing on a small mound of earth that seemed out of place. I was drawn like a magnet to it.

Kneeling with difficulty, it became apparent that the ground had been recently disturbed. I scraped around before I came into contact with a solid object. I began to dig furiously with my bare hands as though someone was egging me on and my very life depended on it.

Carefully I removed a small metal box: it reminded me of a cash box, the type you would keep small change in or objects of minor value. I tugged at the lid, but sadly it was locked. Pulling myself back up, I stood staring.

Scraping off the loose earth I noted traces of black paint now overtaken with rust, also noting the metal hinges were worn and broken. I gave one last tug and the lid gave way. Inside there was an empty compartment with a shallow dish.

I took a deep breath and pulled it out, my eyes focusing on a miniature frame turned upside down, and a small scrap of paper that had begun to disintegrate.

Gingerly I removed the miniature. Turning it over, I gasped, straining my eyes and shaking my head in disbelief. Though badly faded and damaged I was convinced this was a painting of the girl I had seen on the battlements.

I stood for several seconds staring blindly, questioning my reasoning: was it her or was I wishing it was? Placing it carefully in my pocket, I removed the scrap of paper; as I did so more of it disintegrated, but there were still a few legible words.

'We have a love so strong it transcends even death….. Yours forever. Anna x'

'My God,' I whispered to myself, 'such profound words. Right, let's see what Mr James has to say now.'

After replacing the box and re-covering it with earth, my find safely tucked away, I decided to sound out the irritating estate agent, and that if he still would not provide me with an explanation or at least some more in-depth history I would not share them with him.

I negotiated the steep stone stairs once more, entering the second sitting room and calling to Dougy.

'Arh, there you are, Captain, sir. I am in the kitchen with your dog. I must say he does love his fuss.'

Clever man, I thought to myself. Hearts and minds trying to win me over with my dog. Well, give him one more chance then that's it: I will look for other avenues to find out the mystery.

I half-limped into the room, my leg now very painful. This was the most I have walked in months and the wound was objecting to the intrusion.

'So, Mr James, I have had a good look round and I am

interested, but just a few pointers. I know you disagree but I have seen someone on the battlements and heard noises from the house. Damn it, man, the rocking horse in the nursery appeared to be moving.'

'Sadly, Captain, sir as I have already explained, I am the sole keyholder which I trust to no one, not even my staff at the office. I am sure there is a simple explanation, eh, old chap? After all, it's an old house creaking and moving at the seams, so to speak.' He laughed nervously, shuffling awkwardly.

'Anyhow, seen enough for today? Where can I drop you? Will sir be requiring a second viewing?'

CHAPTER 3

The local pub

'Yes please, mid-morning tomorrow final once-over, then I will make my decision. In the meantime please would you be so kind as to take me to that pub in the village?'

The man looked ruffled. 'What, sir? The Ship and Anchor? It's a bit of a dump really. I can recommend you a much nicer place in the next village.'

'No, Mr James, The Ship will do me fine and thank you.'

A few minutes later we pulled up outside the old pub, its timber frame and oak beams twisted and contorted with age, the leaded light windows dark and mysterious, and the single faded hanging sign creaking gently in the sea breeze.

I thanked James and walked the short distance across the cobbled road. To the right was the old harbour, a few fishing boats bobbing gently on the tide. As I reached the open door I called out.

'Why hello, sir. How can I help?' came the kindly reply. 'We are not open for another hour unless, that is, you wish a room for the night.'

I limped in, with Dougy obediently standing to attention at the entrance.

'Why sorry, sir, didn't realise you were military, like, please come in and take a seat by the fire.'

'Ex-, actually, can't get out of the habit of my uniform. Captain Andrew Williamson at your service.' I offered my hand and received a firm grip in return.

'Pleased to meet you. For my sins I am the landlord of this place, Edward Richards, but everyone calls me Ted or Dick. It's a bit too early for a drink, just cleaning the pipes and getting shipshape, so to speak, but I can get me daughter Nancy to make you a nice cuppa with some scones and jam if you fancy.' He paused. 'Oh, she don't speak much these days, just so you know, like.' He pointed a finger to his temple, indicating the lass had a mental problem.

'Oh sorry to hear that, but mmm, tea would be capital, many thanks. Is it all right for my dog to come in? He is no trouble and will just lie by the fire.'

'Yes, of course. Think I have an old bone out the back somewhere.'

Dougy rushed over at my command, making himself comfy in front of the blazing log fire.

'So, couldn't help notice the limp and obviously the patch.'

I contemplated my reply carefully. 'Yes, wounds at Passchendaele I am afraid. In fact been in and out of hospital for three years with these and er, well, other complications.'

'I see. Well, nice bit of Cornish sea air works wonders it do.' He coughed nervously as if not knowing what to say back to me, but then continued. 'I couldn't help notice who dropped you off. You interested in buying the old hall? Been empty for too long – needs some fresh young blood. You have a family, any young 'uns?'

'Well, no, not a present. My fiancée died of the Spanish influenza back in '19, so it's just me, my dog and cat looking for some peace and solitude, then get on with my life. I paint so hereabouts would be wonderful for me, a bit different to my work on the Western Front.' I could feel a panic coming on and lit a cigarette, desperate for a swig from my flask, but decided it was not etiquette to drink one's own alcohol in a licensed premises. I would sneak a crafty one when the landlord disappeared. 'So what can you tell me about the hall? That Mr James is very cagey, almost like he has something to hide.'

'Well, sir, all I can say is I knows a bit, there has been some tragedies that I can tell you, but you need to speak with old Albert, he was born and bred in the village. There's nothing he don't know about anything around here. Be in at 6 on the dot for a pint. Now sorry, must get on with my chores – those pipes won't clean themselves.'

He tipped his cap and walked to the back, calling out for his daughter.

I sat back, letting the warmth from the logs hit my face. Quickly downing a hit of whisky and closing my eyes, I could still see the blurred image of that lowly girl, at the same time reaching in my pocket – yes, the treasures I had unearthed were safe and sound.

I must have dozed off for several minutes and came to with a start because as my eyes focused I was aware there was a young girl standing by my table holding a tray of tea and cakes, coughing politely to get my attention.

I quickly studied the timid figure before thanking her for my tea which she placed carefully on the small cricket table before curtsying and disappearing back behind the bar.

I guessed she was late-teens but more likely early twenties, her face rugged and weather-beaten with a small scar on her cheek. She was pretty, probably just over five feet tall but thin and scrawny. She wore a black skirt with a white blouse covered by a well-worn, almost threadbare, dark cardigan.

My eyes returned to the delightfully presented afternoon tea consisting of a bone china teapot, chrome-coloured strainer, matching cup and saucer, small sugar bowl and a plate of the tastiest-looking scones together with a slice of Victoria sponge.

I called another thankyou but she had already left the bar area. I then proceeded to tuck into my feast, throwing half a scone to Dougy who devoured the pastry before you could blink, licking his lips in approval and staring at me longingly for seconds.

Landlord Ted returned, throwing several logs on the open fire. As the long-case clock chimed 6 he checked the time with a half-hunter draped in his checked waistcoat, then secured the front door open.

'Now sir, I hope you enjoyed your tea. Me missus makes all the food for the pub, she's the best cook for miles and I can vouch for that.' He laughed, tapping his more than ample belly. 'I'll get Nancy to clear your table. Now can I get you something a little stronger?'

'Yes please, a pint of your best with a large whisky.'

'Mm, whisky chaser, my favourite.'

'One for you Ted?'

'No thank very much, bit too early. I stay on the tea until about 9 or I would be too drunk to serve.'

They both laughed.

'Oh will you be eating with us tonight? Best Cornish pasty in the county with me own spuds and veg from the garden.'

'You know what, Ted, I think I will but it's also a bit too early. I'll let you know later what time.'

Again they laughed.

Presently an elderly man entered the bar, striding towards the counter. Ted gave him a warm greeting before enquiring if it was to be the usual. There was a muted conversation, some pointing in my direction. I smiled back.

Presently Ted and the newcomer strolled over to my table.

'So, Captain, this is Albert, the man I was telling you about earlier. He can tell you all you want about the hall.'

I said thankyou. We shook hands and I beckoned him to join me at the table. He had a pint of best bitter in one hand and an unlit pipe in the other, which he placed carefully in the ashtray.

'Please excuse me garb, sir, been working, see.'

I was surprised at this revelation as I put the man at 70 years plus. He was quite tall about 5' 10", dressed in a tweed ticket with patches on the elbows, a striped shirt, minus the collar, and a pair of brown cords held up with a piece of string and tucked into green wellingtons.

'That's fine,' I replied.

'So I hears you are interested in buying Morgwel Hall? It's a crime, you know, been empty all this time.' He paused, supping the beer. 'And Ted explained you wanted some history. Well, lived in this village all my life and worked as gardener up at the hall man and boy, still do one day a week to keep on top of things but it's not really enough. I does me best, anyhow I know it like the back of my hand and all the comings and goings.'

'Perfect,' I replied. 'Well, I have all night if you can spare the time?'

His glass was now empty so I beckoned to the landlord, ordering two whisky chasers, one for me and the other for my new friend. I could see this was to be a long one.

'Why thank you, Captain, sir, that's very generous, thank you kindly. So where would you like me to start?'

'At the beginning please, Albert, at the beginning. Maybe start with just a brief history lesson then tell some more about the family and why they left in such a hurry and of course all the intrigue and comings and goings.' I grinned.

'Wells, sir, lets me think. Well, obviously you can see the castle is a deal older than the hall, built by a local nobleman way back. Bit of a mystery really, not sure what it's there to protect. I mean, there is the harbour and estuary. We think it was probably to keep his family safe in troubled times, anyways it's there.'

He leaned forward, reverting to a whisper. 'You won't have been told this but there is a secret passage from the castle to the cove below which can't be accessed by foot unless there is a really low tide, then you have to paddle. Ideal, see, for...' He paused, scanning the room which was quite empty. '...Smugglers.'

I turned to Ted, pointing for more drinks, lighting a Player's and sat back in anticipation of a marvellous tale. I was indeed hooked and intrigued.

'As far as we know the castle was still occupied in the 1700s. That's when the original manor house was built alongside and connected to it. As legend will have it, the wife of last nobleman living there was barren or had miscarriages, so when they died there was no heir.'

He again paused, supping his beer, now at a slightly slower rate. To my surprise he was still not slurring and very coherent.

'So now where was I? Oh yes. So the place was abandoned, became derelict. No one knew what happened to the money: King George probably got his hands on it, but then in the 19th century by chance the passage to the cove was discovered and then used for smuggling. See, Cornwall is a poor county and people have to make a living somehow. There was the tin mines and fishing but you barely get by.'

'Really, Albert, I am a man of the world: you don't have to explain to me.'

'Wells, sir, so long as you're comfortable with it I will carry on. So everything was going well: the smugglers were bringing in the goods, the locals could afford cheap baccy and spirits, but one night there was a terrible storm. They managed to get ashore and were bringing the contraband through the passage to the ruins when Customs officers sprang their trap. There were about fifteen or so men in the group: they fought back but were vastly outnumbered by the Queen's men who opened fire, killing some in the ruins. Others were trapped in the tiny passage and were also killed. As the story goes, whoever was left put back to sea in the boat but the storm claimed the rest of them. It's a sad, true story.'

He took another sup of his beer, again looking around the room. 'Legend has it you can still hear the screams of the smugglers trapped in the passage. In fact, I myself have heard them, though there is a lot of non-believers. I swear on my oath it's all true.'

'Now then, Albert, don't you be telling your ghost stories to the gentleman, he may well end up living there,' ventured landlord Ted. 'I think maybe it's the drink making your stories a bit too far-fetched.'

'Thays not stories, Ted, and I is not affected by the drink. Even if I was, it is what it is, and it's true: the place is definitely haunted. Anyways, it was left to ruin until the Westlake family, very wealthy people, mines, tea, sugar, farming, you names it, they were into it. Wells, now see they bought it and rebuilt what's now the present manor house that you see. Now that was about 1850: they moved in and lived very happily for a time, but for all their money let me tell you they was a troubled family and things began to go wrong.'

At that juncture I decided to keep the eerie happenings and findings I had experienced to myself and let Albert continue, as I didn't want to encourage him to embellish his tale: I wanted facts.

Albert supped his beer then lit his pipe, deep in thought before continuing. 'Listen, young man, don't take any notice of Ted. Nows I am not saying the place is or isn't haunted: all depends on what you believe, like. All I knows is there were some grim goings-on and strange things still occur. Best I tell it all then you make up your own mind.'

I was fast liking this quirky man with his broad Cornish accent and the way he often added an s to his words, and I was now completely fascinated by the history of Morgwel Hall.

I nodded in agreement, then in the next instant Nancy approached with the pasty together with the accompanying potatoes and veg, Ted calling out that he hoped I didn't mind but was stopping food in the next few minutes. I nodded and smiled, mouthing a thankyou to the timid girl.

Albert had left the table for the gents. The girl looked around nervously then slid a piece of paper towards me, shaking her head and putting a finger to her mouth. I understood then she turned and was gone.

I studied the paper which I read from the table. 'Please sir, I need to speak to you urgently about the hall, there are things that even Albert does not know'. Then I pushed it safely into my pocket as the old gardener returned.

'I am sorry.' I gestured to the food. 'Would you like to join me?'

He looked at the tavern clock. 'No thank ye, though that's indeed very kind but me missus will already be cross on account of me being so late. Dinner be in the oven: I dare not tell I have dined out or she will skin me alive.'

I grinned, beckoning him to continue whilst I ate.

'Mm, so where was we? Oh yes. So, as I say, it was the Westlake family who rebuilt the manor house. Apparently it took about three years before they moved in and as you know reconnected it to the old castle. Now let me think, there was the father Augustus, his wife Charlotte, son Thomas, he was a bugger – well, actually, so was the father. Now you must bear in mind that these stories are second-hand. I was a nipper when they first lived there, but I did know them obviously as I became the gardener.'

He stopped again, supping the last of his beer and downing the whisky deep in thought. 'So anyways it was an unhappy marriage. Augustus spent his time drinking, womanising and gambling, while his poor wife became even more withdrawn and reclusive. The son was sent away for education. Now hims was a very bright one, though played up a bit being at boarding school.'

I beckoned to Ted for another drink; this time Albert declined.

'That's very kind but I best be getting off in a couple of minutes. Just finish up then maybe continue tomorrow, same time if you wish. I knows a lot more about the present owners. So it was very sad: Mrs Charlotte was sent away to a recovery home, though methinks it was an asylum, then Augustus buried himself in his self-destruction, squandering vast amounts of the family fortune. We was then told she died, but it's a common belief that he just disowned his wife, then suddenly he dropped dead from a heart attack, so Thomas as the only son inherited: luckily he was very shrewd and over the next few years managed to build up the business, once again restoring the fortunes. He threw lavish parties, loved the ladies, then one day he met and married his wife Miss Evelyn: now, she was a gem.'

The pub was now virtually empty with only one other at the bar. When the clock struck the half-hour I remember poor Albert jumping with a start. 'Blimey, Captain, sir, where has that time gone? Best be off, tomorrow all right with you?'

'Yes, of course, can't wait.' I shook his hand as he exited the bar. My taxi driver appeared to take me back to the hotel in Penzance: my mind was racing.

'Landlord, bill please, and do you have a room for tomorrow? I think I want to stay in the village and near to Morgwel.'

'Why of course, sir, it would be our honour, though we are quite a humble establishment, nothing grand, hope it suits. I will get Nancy to make ready the best room: the windows overlook the harbour. Also a couple of comfortable easy chairs and a small desk. The bathroom is right next door. No one else staying at present so it's all yours, so to speak.'

I thanked Ted, settling the money, leaving a generous tip, said my goodbyes then climbed aboard the automobile for the ride to my hotel. I remember piecing together the mystery of the Westlake family and being full of excitement and expectation for the following day.

CHAPTER 4

My night was quite restless. I tossed and turned, the image of the girl on the tower embedded in my mind, then I would drift into a gentle doze to be woken by the sounds of the screams from the castle passage, the gently moving rocking horse becoming a wild stallion; then my whisky would calm me.

At some point I must have drifted off, for a sudden sharp knock at the bedroom door brought me around. 'Sorry, sir, to bother you,' said the voice from behind the timber panels, 'but you requested an early morning call. It's 7.30, breakfast is served at your convenience. Thank you.'

I rubbed my eyes, slowly coming to life. The previous evening I had purposely left the curtains slightly open and now the brilliant light of a new day streamed in. I yawned and stretched my leg, painful from the night's inactivity.

I turned to look at my silver travelling clock, at the same time taking that day's first hit of whisky. Moving from the bed I could see it was a dull, blustery day with deep black rain clouds threatening to open at any moment.

My suite had a separate living space plus its own facilities. I began to run a bath, the water splashing gently on its sides and the steam quickly filling the air. My shaving set was ready by the basin. I was relishing the day, but also holding a deal of apprehension, plus, as ridiculous as it seems, I could feel myself falling in love with the girl on the tower, or at least an inexplicable attraction. Was I going mad again?

Rising from the calming, hot waters I rubbed at the misted mirror before using my badger brush to whip up a creamy foam for my shave, then gently pulling the blade across my cheeks, the hard stubble rasping in unison.

Selecting a freshly pressed uniform, I checked myself in the full-length mirror, gave my hair a last-minute lick, then descended to the restaurant where I demolished a full Cornish. I knew it would be a long, arduous day.

I had arranged to meet Mr James at the house, rather than having to endure his incessant drivel on the drive there, plus I wanted to be there at least an hour before him. A local taxi firm ferried me with no fuss, then he was to drop my kit off at The Ship and Anchor.

After paying off the man I stood staring at the battlements with Dougy sitting at my feet awaiting orders, then from behind a bush I heard the voice of a young girl. 'Captain, sir, Captain, it's me from The Ship pub. How long will we be alone?'

I turned, facing her with my inquisitive look. 'Young lady, I am mystified. I was told you no longer speak.'

She went bright red. 'Well, sorry, sir, actually I don't much since my traumas but I can in fact. It's not that I can't, it's that I am, how shall I put it…?' She paused in thought. 'Ah yes, selective whom I speak with, and anyhow it stops any unwanted questions into my past. Also everyone thinks I am a bit stupid and can't read or write but I can and good, see.'

'Well, that's fine with me, I know all about traumas.' I paused. A slight sweat was breaking out. I fumbled in my jacket pocket to ensure the flask was to hand. 'Anyhow, that's another story,' I said quickly before changing the subject. 'Oh and I must say that was the most delicious meal last night.'

She smiled, leaning forward to give Dougy his much-loved fuss and right on cue he rolled onto his back, all four legs reaching towards the sky and enjoying the attention from this new admirer.

'So, Captain, what do you think of Morgwel?' She gestured towards the magnificent building that was outlined against the grey skyline.

'Well, young lady, I absolutely love it, though don't want to appear too keen to that estate agent Mr James.'

She laughed. 'You're going to make an offer, then?'

'Still debating. Need another conference with my dog before the final decision, but yes more than likely, especially if I can have a good deal, hence playing it down.'

She smiled.

'You know, Miss Richards, I hope you don't mind me saying but you have the loveliest smile and you speak so eloquently. None of my business of course, but seems a shame for such a lovely voice not to be heard more often.'

She blushed. 'Why thank you, kindly sir, but I would prefer to be called Nancy, that's if you don't mind? As for the speaking, well, maybe I will share my reasons properly with you one day.'

'So, Nancy, you know some secrets about the hall?'

'Well, sir, yes, I mean there's quite a lot of mystery and conjecture but I also have a lot of facts. You see, I worked here part-time but my best friend and her mother were permanent staff, like, lived in the servants' quarters next to the kitchen.' She seemed to become saddened at the mention of her friend, her eyes looking aimlessly to the drive before continuing. 'But whatever I tells thee I don't want it to put you off buying.'

I smiled. 'I can assure you nothing will, so please carry on.'

Suddenly Dougy leapt up, running to the base of the battlements, his tail tucked firmly between his legs, ears forward, fur ruffled and barking for all he was worth. I instinctively looked towards the tower and was convinced I saw the grey shawl disappear behind the wall.

I remember running to the front door but it was definitely locked. I ran back looking, searching the castle ruins, but nothing.

'Sir, what is it? Everything all right?'

I again decided to keep my experiences at the hall to myself, quickly conjuring up a story. 'What? Oh yes, fine. Sorry, I think there must be a cat there, Dougy always chases them. Still, gone now.' She seemed happy with my explanation.

'I know, my friend's dog is the same: peaceful as anything but sees a cat and changes instantly.'

I stood motionless for several seconds, desperate for a glimpse of 'her', but the battlements remained empty. Dougy returned to us, tail now wagging in the hope of more fuss, then Nancy continued.

'So, Captain, as I was saying, my best friend's mum worked

here most of her life. She was a widow, like, but then when she was old enough, Elsa, that's my friend's name, she also worked for the Westlakes. It was a tough life, let me tell you, but the master was more than fair and allowed her out at least every two weeks, sometimes more. We would walk for miles along the beaches, sometimes borrow a couple of ponies that were grazing, they were a bit old, like, so the owners didn't mind. Now that was fun, we would gallop bareback along the cliff down to the river at low tide, then along the beach back to the fields and a lovely picnic.' She paused. 'Please don't say anything to my dad but I used to raid the pub fridge, you know pasties and stuff, like: thems were wonderful times.' She hesitated, looking uncomfortable. As I studied her changing demeanour I was sure there were tears in her eyes. 'Thens, well… thens it all changed. Elsa wasn't so much fun, made excuses not to come out. She looked tired and drawn, I didn't like it, but she would not tell me what was wrong which also upset me. We never, I mean never, had any secrets from each other. Then one day I was waiting for her at our secret meeting spot. She arrived sobbing, covering a black eye. Her face was red as though she had been slapped.'

Suddenly I heard a car approaching the gravel drive, giving their pending arrival away. I looked at my watch: if that was the agent he was half an hour early.

'Oh my word!' screamed Nancy. 'If that's Mr James he will skin me alive for talking to you. I must go.'

I turned towards the sound of the approaching car then back to Nancy to explain that I would ask to again be left alone in the house, but she had disappeared. 'Damn and blast,' I mumbled to myself. 'Damn and blast.'

I dusted myself down, preparing to meet the ever more irritating man. He stepped from the car and had obviously not spotted me. 'Mr James, sir, you're early,' I said, looking at my wristwatch.

I startled him. 'Goodness, Captain, you made me jump. Yes, thought I would unlock ready for your inspection. Any more thoughts as to an offer?'

'All in good time, man. I really am not sure, I need to spend more time here today and alone again if you please.' This time I waved five notes at the man which he eagerly grabbed, stuffing them quickly into his inside jacket breast pocket.

I still had not explored fully the outside area and made a mental note that was to be on my list of 'to dos'. Presently James returned, informing me that all was unlocked, including the passage to the tower. I thanked him profusely, then together with Dougy entered Morgwel for the second time.

Mr James called after me. 'What time shall I return, sir?'

I asked him to give me a few hours as I really wanted to savour the atmosphere.

After hearing Nancy's story I made my way to the kitchen and found a door towards the end of a small corridor that I had missed on yesterday's visit. On the opposite side was another door: this appeared to lead outside and at the end an ascending spiral staircase, which I surmised was used by servants.

Pushing the door open gingerly, I peered inside. It was a small sitting room, an open fire, some basic furniture, cobbled flooring. The atmosphere was cold and damp: on the far side were three doors. I ventured cautiously in, walking slowly across the floor and stopping outside the first.

Turning the brass handle, the old timbers creaked as I pushed it fully open. Inside was a single Victorian metal bedstead, a small chest of drawers, old, rusty hanging rail, and finally a tin washbasin sitting on a dilapidated dressing table. I shivered.

The next two doors revealed the same, though one room was slightly bigger and was obviously a little more comfortable, a double bed against the wall with the mattress still in place but looking grubby and uninviting. I deduced that this was the servants' living quarters probably where Nancy's friend and mother would have resided.

Having satisfied my curiosity, I felt armed with more information to have a better understanding when the young girl would resume her tale; but for me, I was eager to climb the old castle to the battlements.

Making my way back through the house to the second living room, I noted that the door to the ruins had been opened by Mr James. I looked in to make sure the coast was clear, my military training kicking in. Dougy scampered in at full flight, bounding up the stone stairs and soon disappearing.

I followed at my own pace, my leg still very stiff and indeed giving me a lot of pain. It's strange, I had only been there once but the place seemed very familiar and dare I say I was feeling more at home as each minute ticked by.

I stopped before the final flight to the outside, gaining my breath. Dougy was barking frantically; I needed a hit of whisky. Fumbling in my pocket I came upon the miniature that had slipped my memory.

Pulling it out I examined the painting, admiring the beauty that I assumed was Anna, but who was she? Why was this buried in the castle? I still hadn't fully cleaned the glass and decided, whilst catching my breath, that was a good job to be done.

Taking out my silk hanky I spat on the glass, apologising to the girl for being so rude, but then as I rubbed and more of the painting became visible I gasped, crying out loud, 'My God, no, it can't be?!' but sure enough, as God's my witness, I could just make out a grey shawl.

I searched frantically for my hip flask, taking three hits one after the other, again bringing the miniature into my sight. Yes, I had not imagined it: there it was, a grey shawl covering the girl's delicate shoulders, only just in view but enough that I was sure.

I was brought back to earth by Dougy's barking, then suddenly, tail between his legs this time, squealing, he ran past me, descending the stairs. I called for him to halt but to no avail.

The final few steps were a real chore but eventually I was greeted by light streaming in through the entrance. One last effort and I was there. I stopped dead in my tracks, rubbing my eyes, for there behind the thorns was the girl. This time I saw her for a few seconds: she was looking out to sea.

I gasped, rubbing my eyes and calling out, but when I looked, as previously, she had simply disappeared into thin air.

I stood still for several minutes surveying the castle

ramparts where I had just seen the lady in the grey shawl, before limping over to the exact spot where she was standing. Turning, I looked at the vista: the view of the sea from this point was truly breathtaking and encompassed the whole bay.

I scanned from left to right: the glorious blue water with its foam edges stretched into infinity from sandy cove to battered rocks and cliff-lines, then back to the harbour which I could just make out, the narrow entrance beginning to fill with the incoming tide.

I lit a cigarette and leaned on my stick, resisting the temptation for a hit from the flask. No, I had had enough already that morning and if I was to proceed with an offer didn't want a fuzzy head to hinder my negotiating skills.

Dougy had returned and was sitting patiently, his deep brown eyes staring intently at me: he seemed to be quite calm and was waiting for my orders.

'Come on, boy, let's go outside. Don't really need to see much more. I think pretty soon we will be calling Morgwel our new home. Then we can really have an exploration that's going to be part of the fun discovering new things about this place.'

As I turned to leave, instead, on an impulse, I turned back, deciding to sketch the castle battlements, pulling out a folded artists' paper and pencil I always kept with me for such an eventuality. I carefully re-created the scene and of course added the mystery lady. I have no logical explanation of my next actions.

I went on to sign my masterpiece, 'Captain Williamson with love to Anna', adding a single kiss, carefully placing the drawing on the spot where she had been standing and securing it with four hefty stones, thus ensuring it would not be blown away.

'Right, boy, now we can go. Come on, I can't wait to see the grounds: there are acres, cliff edges, a small lake with babbling brook, and let's find the path to our very own private sandy cove.'

Dougy wagged his tale in agreement, though logically he didn't have a clue what I was talking about. I laughed to myself: talking to dogs like they are humans dedicating sketches to. I stopped myself: who or what did I dedicate the drawing to? Certainly no one could just vanish as she does, then decided I was thinking too deeply.

Having seen the mystery lady complete in her grey shawl seemed to put a sparkle into my day, also coming to the conclusion that I was not in fact mad for I had spotted her on more than one occasion, but still with the intention of keeping all this to myself until I had built up the whole picture.

I walked through the front door in the hope that young Nancy had returned, even calling her name, but alas she had obviously been frightened off. Still, at least I would see her at The Ship that evening and possibly be able to arrange another liaison.

The day passed quickly. Together with Dougy I covered the remains of the house and the grounds, deciding to leave the cove for another day. I was sitting outside adjacent to the front door when Mr James pulled up.

'Seen enough, Captain, sir? Shall I lock up?'

'Yes that's fine. I have, thank you.'

He quickly secured the property, finally closing and locking the front door.

'So, Captain, sir, where do we go from here? Do you think an offer is in the pipeline?'

'Tell you what, Mr James, let's go back to The Ship and talk.'

He smiled, opening the rear door for me and Dougy, trying his best to be civil to my dog but when he thought I wasn't looking, frowning in disgust. I laughed to myself. Want my money, old man? You have to accept both me and the dog.

CHAPTER 5

We arrived shortly at the inn, selecting a private table and chairs by the front window. Landlord Ted was busy about his chores but quickly arranged for tea and cakes to be brought over. I lit a cigarette, trying to act nonchalant.

'So let's get down to business, eh, Mr James? Firstly, forget the asking price. £25,000 guineas is quite exorbitant, I only work in pounds so the start is £25,000 (approx a million in today's money). Agree?'

I could see he was not expecting that. He coughed nervously, explaining that he only had discretionary powers of negotiation but he did agree to pounds. Mm, too quick, I thought: he has a lot of power but is holding out for his client, as he should.

'So, Mr James, here is my offer.' I paused. '£20,000: take it or leave it.'

The poor man almost choked on his tea, replying instantly that the offer was an insult.

'Why, Mr Westlake has already turned down more than that.'

I studied the man carefully. He was not good at this – probably more used to selling small cottages and the like. This type of money did not come into play that often in this part of Cornwall.

'Come now, Captain, a sensible offer if you please.'

I was trying desperately not to let my heart rule my head but I didn't want to lose the place.

'Fine, well, let me explain. I am a cash buyer and could have the funds transferred, well, immediately. The lawyers are done I have a chambers in London who can proceed very quickly.' I paused. 'Just think of that large commission cheque, eh, Mr James?'

The man had beads of sweat trickling down his face and neck which he quickly wiped with a hanky. He looked cautiously about the room, leaning forward. 'I shouldn't really be telling you this, Captain, but you seem like a man of honour. Between you and me that is the absolute lowest Mr Westlake will go to: been on the market for two years and no real offers, but I will still have to just confirm with him 100%. I will go into the post office in Penzance and try to telephone him. If not, it will be a telegram.'

He rose, shook my hand then was gone. I looked at my watch: still two hours before the bar was open but ample time for James to return, with hopefully good news, I remember checking that Ted was not around and snuck a quick secret celebratory snifter from the flask.

Nancy nervously approached my table. 'Sorry about this morning, sir, but if that Mr James knew I had been telling you the stories, well, my life would have been hell.'

'Nancy, don't worry, I have bought the place and look forward to a visit and hearing more of your prose. Anyhow, tonight gardener Albert is meeting me so I imagine there will be more than enough to be going on with.'

'Well, Captain, sir, that is good news.' She smiled. 'But there are still some dark secrets I believe you should know, but I will look forward to visiting you real soon.' With that, she cleared the table and was gone.

At 5.30 on the dot Mr James returned, his face beaming. 'Managed to get hold of Mr Westlake, Captain, sir, and he has accepted your offer so please let's shake hands to seal the deal.'

I beamed, Dougy even letting out a yap of approval as if in recognition. But little was I to know the can of worms and findings that I was to open once I moved into the hall.

I called to the landlord for some champagne: even though he was not officially open, he selected a bottle and kindly poured three glasses. I insisted he join in the toast. James downed his quickly to return to his office and ensure the sale process was in motion.

I sat back, quietly tugging on a Player's, patiently waiting for Albert to return and continue with his tales, but sadly he did not make an appearance that night.

Having feasted on locally caught grilled fish, accompanied with chips, I decided to turn in for the evening, explaining to landlord Ted that I had an early start the following day and needed to be in Penzance for the milk train to Paddington. He kindly organised my cab.

I also explained that I would be returning shortly, would let him know the dates and for him to please give Albert a message that I would require his services as gardener and was looking forward to learning more of the history of my new home.

I slept well that night, the combination of good food, alcohol and the satisfying, comforting knowledge that I had secured my piece of Heaven on earth, but also relishing the thought of unravelling the mystery of the hall.

CHAPTER 6

My journey back to London was uneventful, but quite slow and tedious. I had secured a first-class carriage, which remained empty apart from myself and Dougy. I tried to read but in the end amused myself by studying the stunning English countryside and trying to identify station names as we flashed by.

As we approached the outskirts of the capital I noted how the scenery was changing as urbanisation had begun its sprawl, and the train had slowed considerably. By the time we stopped at Paddington I was quite tired and, even though I had managed several walks around the carriages I was in considerable pain from my old leg wound.

I had previously arranged for a private dog sitter, who was also looking after Willy, my cat, to collect Dougy from the station, as sadly the Savoy did not have any facilities for pets. On seeing the man, Dougy began to wag his tail and after some hasty fuss I handed him over.

My cab dropped me at the Savoy where I had booked rooms for a few weeks and was staying prior to my Cornish jaunt, two busboys running to secure my luggage, of which I must confess there was little – well, compared to the kit I had upstairs.

I stepped wearily into my room and ran a bath, deciding

to soak in the delicious warm waters before taking an early dinner. I would speak with my lawyers the next day to ascertain the time period before I owned Morgwel.

I was now no longer a member of the Army, having recently resigned my commission, the letter of confirmation arriving the day I left for Cornwall. Tonight was to be a first for me: no uniform, just a plan old dinner suit. I was feeling strangely nervous.

The warmth of the water combined with a mix of bath salts recommend by my doctor were working their miracle on my leg wound; then as I relaxed, the image of the girl in the grey shawl returned to me. I smiled to myself, more content than for many years.

I dried myself, checking in the mirror. I had quite a six o'clock shadow and decided on a second shave that day; having finished, now wrapped in my dressing gown I sat in one of the large leather sofas surveying the room.

What a contrast to my humble lodgings at The Ship and Anchor. I had a large bedroom with sofa, connecting bathroom and a sitting room overlooking the Strand, large windows with grand drapes, plus a scattering of fine rugs, and in the corner a small writing bureau. It was luxurious beyond but I knew where I would prefer to be.

I sat for several minutes studying the throng of cabs, each battling for position and custom, some dropping off smartly dressed gents at the hotel. I noted one couple arriving in a Rolls-Royce, their chauffeur dressed in fine livery.

As I stood to dress myself I felt one of my 'deep coughs'

coming on. I fumbled for a hanky then from the depths of my chest I convulsed, a single droplet of searing red blood contrasting on the brilliant white cotton.

I cursed to myself.

Back in 1915 I was stationed in Loos for a brief period and in September I was to witness and help as we launched our first gas attack in retaliation for one the Germans had executed earlier that year. But the wind changed direction and blew it back to our lines.

I remember the warning bells sounding up and down the line; at that time we had only rudimentary protection and those without were told to piss on their hankies and breathe through them.

I looked in utter disbelief as the deadly cloud shifted direction directly towards our position.

My mask was no more that cotton impregnated with chemicals and clamped to my face, together with goggles to protect my eyes; then as the cloud hit I heard many screams as men were swamped by the deadly mass.

I remember vividly a young lad, no more that 16 or 17, running to a shell hole for what he thought was better protection. I tried to warn him that the gas would lie there, but to no avail: the next second he was screaming, tearing at his own eyes.

It was panic, pandemonium: men coughing, screaming as the mist swirled its death all around. Another young boy was running half-blinded by the gas; he hadn't seen me and we collided with force. As he fell to the ground grabbing wildly, he pulled my mask to one side – not for long, a split second, but enough for me to gulp in a small amount of the vile vapour.

I hastily secured my protection but could already feel a burning sensation in my throat. I fought for breath through the cotton mask, panicking, sweat now pouring from my forehead, stinging my eyes, and the pain in my lungs like a piece of shrapnel hitting flesh.

I fell to my knees, desperate to tear off the mask and breathing deeper and faster. From the corner of my eye I saw a medic approaching, his voice muffled by a mask. I had no idea what he was saying, then I passed out.

The next I remember was clean, white sheets and a nurse bending over my bed. She comforted me, reminding me how lucky I had been.

The London specialist whom I attended for help with my breathing had told me that I would always have a weakness, but my lungs were now working at almost full capacity, though he couldn't promise how I would fare as I grew older. Sadly, though now six years on, I would from time to time still cough up blood. This was one such occasion, a sickening reminder of a terrifying time......

I stood in front of the full-length mirror hating my formal dinner suit, thinking I looked more like a penguin than a gentleman of substance. I quickly changed into my dress uniform, at once becoming at ease.

I elected to have a quick drink at the bar before taking my place at The Grill, ordering a large malt whisky from their impressive selection. It was very early in the evening and

I was almost alone. I surveyed the scene, firstly observing a table with four gents talking and pointing at paperwork, a grand-looking couple supping champagne, and another man dressed in an officer's uniform enjoying a smoke and a beer. We acknowledged each other with a nod, with me praying he would not venture over, for I needed to be alone.

In the semi-darkness of a secluded corner a young couple were canoodling, holding hands, also supping champagne. 'What was their story?' I wondered. A number of waiters were hovering in the background.

The bar was solid, wooden panelling with a marble top. Behind the counter were two men dressed in dinner suits busily polishing glasses. The lighting was dim and atmospheric, with a scattering of tables, some laid for two others set for four, littering the gleaming timber flooring.

In the background from the main restaurant a trio of musicians played a selection of soft, melodic tunes which gently entered the bar, the smoke from cigarettes floating to the ceiling and seeming to be dancing in rhythm.

After a short period I was approached by a man, probably in his thirties, smartly dressed in dinner suit, a notepad in one hand and a menu in the other. He informed me my table was ready and asked if I would prefer to order at the bar whilst enjoying my pre-dinner drink.

I decided to stay seated and began to study the menu, eventually choosing soup of the day and a sirloin steak. I would not order wine, instead staying with my malt. The waiter returned, taking note of my selection for that evening. I ordered another drink.

A few minutes later he returned, placing my glass on a tray and asking me to follow him to the restaurant, showing me politely to my table. It was perfect, tucked out of the way next to the wall, a huge pot plant slightly obscuring me.

As I sat waiting for my first course I closed my eyes, picturing my deceased fiancée Lizzie. We had dined at the Savoy Grill on one of our first dates. Then curiously my mind drifted to the girl from Cornwall, smiling, laughing, her beauty becoming more apparent. Suddenly I longed to be back at my new home seeking her out.

I rubbed my eyes and shook my head. Of course I was alone. I grabbed my whisky, eagerly downing the remains of it and also lighting a Player's. What was happening me?

The soup was top-notch, then as I sat back awaiting my mains, from the corner of my eye I spotted a uniform. On looking closer I realised it was Colonel Roberts, the commanding officer of my former regiment. 'Damn and blast, he has spotted me,' I whispered.

'Williams, Williams, is that you, old son?'

The smart, tall man all but ran towards my table, closely followed by his meek and downtrodden wife Verity. I had only met her on a few occasions, mainly at regimental balls. She sadly lived very much in the colonel's shadow, almost bullied by the man, though for all that he was a first-rate officer.

I rose from my chair, saluting, then offered my hand. 'Why, Colonel, absolutely delighted: it's been, well, a couple of years at least.'

'Williams, old man, so good to see you. Of course you remember my wife?'

'Yes, sir, delighted to make your acquaintance once more, Mrs Roberts. Now, if I remember correctly, you were a dab hand at the foxtrot.'

The poor women blushed. 'Well, Captain, you have a good memory but I seem to remember, though, you having two left feet.'

It was my turn to blush but we all laughed.

'So Williams, how was that place in Scotland and what you up to now? I see you're in uniform but aren't you a civvy?'

'Yes, sir, hope you don't mind. Can't get used to not wearing it and let's just say Scotland has helped me through.'

'Why no, of course I don't.' He turned to his wife. 'Wounded three times, my dear, three times. Very brave man, even awarded a gong if I remember, at the third battle of Ypres.'

I hated all the pomp and fuss that had been made of what I termed my duty, though I did wear the medal with much pride.

'So, you still in the family business? So sad to hear of your parents' demise, awful tragedy, but I surmise you inherited and will be running it.'

'Well, actually, sir, I have sold the lot, retaining minor shareholdings. Invested the money in property and other boring things, no need to work. In fact just bought a manor house in Cornwall where I intend to paint. Might even buy another farm.'

'What?' exclaimed the somewhat pompous man. 'With all

your business acumen? Still, if that is what you want. Mind you, damn good with the brushes. Did some blooming good images of our battles.'

From the entrance I noted uniforms with more brass, gold and medals than an entire brigade.

'Ah, the rest of my party. Anyhow, Williams, so nice to have seen you again. Oh and good luck. Maybe send me one of those paintings, eh?' He turned, hurrying to his guests.

'It's bloody Williamson, sir. You always get it wrong,' I thought to myself, relieved that they had left me.

The mention of my parents' deaths brought alive another memory that I had buried. They were passengers on a liner to New York that was torpedoed by Germans, and along with all hands perished at sea.

The business was diverse but centred on a huge arable farm, though we didn't live there, and during the war my father expanded our munitions and engineering divisions, with many lucrative Army contracts. But I wanted none of it: I needed peace, to paint and find the girl in the grey shawl.

My steak was delicious, which I devoured eagerly. I said no to pudding, feeling the need to control my waistline. The waiter approached: I signed the chit and asked if he would be so kind as to send a bottle of Glenmorangie to my room, at the same time slipping him a handsome tip.

I sat in my living room enjoying the malt, simply watching the traffic on the Strand, the many lights dazzling, honking of horns, people going hither and thither about their business. I must have dozed off, alcohol-induced, as I awoke with a start and a shiver just before 3 a.m., somehow finding my bed, then once more drifted off.

CHAPTER 7

At 8.30 on the dot there was a knock on my door, with a loud voice calling that breakfast was served. I had quite forgotten that I had ordered room service the previous evening. I pulled on my gown and allowed the two waiters in: they set out my table like a banquet.

I tucked into the lavish spread then readied myself for the forthcoming day. My appointment with my lawyers was scheduled for 11.00 a.m. at Lincoln's Inn Fields. I could hardly contain my excitement.

I quickly bathed and shaved, again donning my uniform. Descending the stairs to the grand foyer, I enquired if there was any mail for me. There wasn't so I asked for a bellboy to flag me down a cab, though generally there was always at least one waiting outside.

The short journey was covered quickly. I alighted, paying the talkative driver before heading for law firm Stevens, Stevens and Stevens. Perhaps at this juncture I should explain the name.

The firm consists of three brothers, the youngest partner an old pal of mine from Cambridge. They were good and trustworthy, and I liked to support them, though in fact their reputation was excellent and they had built up a good clientele.

As I waited in the smart reception I studied the various certificates and qualifications interspersed with a pleasant surprise to me: a number of my wartime paintings from the trenches.

'Andrew, old chap, it's been too long,' boomed the voice of my friend William Stevens. I smiled and we shook hands.

'Yes, old friend, too long and golly, I feel honoured.' I pointed to the paintings.

'No, old man, it's us that are honoured that we own them and have put them on display. Lest we forget, eh? But anyhow, how's your health? The leg, eye and well, you know, how was Scotland?'

'Well, thanks, I am fine, well, recovered. My leg still gives me gyp, my eye does pain on occasion and my breathing, well, that's under control and my jaunt up North – don't really want to talk about it.'

'No, of course not. Come, let me show you my new office.'

I followed William through a small maze of passageways, passing a room with several women busily typing, and finally reaching his very plush office. His desk was huge with two chairs to the front and his a massive leather job. Towards a window was a leather Chesterfield and two matching armchairs, a number of filing cabinets, and net curtains drawn back, revealing a pleasing view to the grass 'park' of Lincoln's Inn.

'My word, haven't you done well? Oh and I must thank you again for handling all my business affairs and the like.'

'Well, I should maybe thank you: that was a handsome

cheque for our time. Why did you up it?'

'Why? Because I knew you were undercharging me, as a friend, and it didn't feel right.'

'Very gracious, I must say.'

'So what news on my purchase?'

My friend didn't reply immediately; instead I felt he was studying me intently.

'Before I continue I feel I need to ask you something as a friend, nay, a bloody good friend.' He paused: I was all ears. 'It's just that, well, are you sure this is the right move for you, you know, after all you have been through? I mean Cornwall, as lovely as it is, well, it's such a long way away. What about your friends and the like? Please don't think I am talking out of turn, it's just, well, I am concerned.'

I could feel a sweat approaching. Delving into my pocket I felt my hip flask, if needed, which gave me some comfort. I thought carefully about my reply.

'Firstly, thanks for your concern but I can assure you this is not a hasty decision. I have spent a long time thinking this through, which in hospital I had plenty of opportunity to do, and yes, it's right for me.' I paused. 'I really don't enjoy, well, all this, London and everything that goes with it. I need peace and solitude. Anyhow, Cornwall is ideal for me to paint. I might even purchase another farm, oh and in case you don't know, it's only a few hours away by train.'

We laughed.

There was a knock at the door. 'Sorry to bother you, sir, but I need to collect any correspondence you need posting to catch the lunchtime pick-up,' came the request from a young office boy.

William looked around his desk, gathering together several letters and handing them to the waiting youngster.

I took this opportunity to excuse myself. 'William, sorry, have you a gents, please?'

'Of course. Turn left down the corridor, a couple of doors along.'

I hurried from my chair, the panic erupting from the depths of my stomach. Pushing open the door marked 'Men Only', I selected a cubicle and quickly downed a hit from my flask, instantly feeling calmer.

Once back in the office I continued. 'No, seriously, William it's a different pace of life, people very friendly. I have in fact already made some acquaintances as well.' I hesitated then without thinking blurted out, 'Oh and yes, I have met someone,' immediately regretting my foolish outburst.

William raised his eyebrows. 'Well, really, old man, you're a bit of a dark horse, eh? So tell me all about her.'

'Sorry, William, really should not have said anything, it's still early days,' I stuttered.

'Oh come on, what's her name, what's she look like, what are her circumstances?'

I felt myself blush. 'As I said, old friend, it's very early days so I will tell all in good time. Now to business: how is my purchase looking?'

He shuffled some papers before looking directly at me with a huge smile. 'Well, you're a lucky bugger, turns out Mr

Westlake is in town, his London lawyers have the deeds and the like, just a few more enquiries from my side, transfer the funds on your say-so and well, that's it, Morgwel can be yours by the end of the week.'

I beamed. 'Capital news, William, capital. Now I must get organised: where do I sign?'

We quickly dispensed with the remaining paperwork before taking a short stroll to William's club where we enjoyed a light lunch, celebrating my impending purchase with a bottle of champagne, after which we shook hands and I returned to the hotel, my mind in a whirl.

After confirming with William that I was not needed for more paperwork and that in an emergency they had a limited power of attorney, I had decided to head back to Cornwall the following day if I could tie up any loose ends.

The hotel kindly sent a messenger to my pet 'babysitters' in Bow, and also booked a first-class ticket from Paddington on the mid-morning express, arriving at Penzance late afternoon. I then telegraphed The Ship and Anchor to ready my room, speculating that landlord Ted would be the talk of the village, as I imagine there were not too many sent in that part of the country.

By the time I had completed all my tasks I was exhausted and decided on a long soak, a quick early evening pre-dinner drink in the bar, followed by room service. I had seen enough people today to last me a lifetime.

As I sat in the cavernous bath my mind drifted to Cornwall and the house. I felt a sudden twinge of excitement at the thought of my new life. Then I thought of her, the beautiful girl that seemed so carefree, dancing in the battlements. My stomach became knotted.

It was just after 5.00pm when I entered the empty bar, selecting a stool at the end. The friendly barman greeted me with a smile, enquiring what my tipple was to be for the evening.

I carefully examined the row of malts. 'Tell you what, Bert, you choose for me.' I smiled and lit a Player's.

'Now, sir, this is one of my favourites,' he said, pointing to a darkish-coloured bottle.' It's a micro-distillery on a tiny island off the coast of Scotland. They only produce a small amount each year and ration it to their customers: we receive only six bottles. It's quite light but there is a peaty taste normally associated with heavy malts. See what you think.'

He gave me a mini-taster glass, pouring a small amount of the insipid-looking liquid. I swirled it around, sniffing the strong odour before sipping it. I gave an approving look. 'Well, Bert, good choice: that's one of the best ever. Can I pay for one when you finish your shift?'

'No, sir, that won't be necessary, but thank you anyway, just you enjoy it.'

He handed me a full glass which I sipped eagerly.

A waiter approached, asking if I required a table for the evening. I declined and gave him my room service order, asking for it to be delivered at about 6 o'clock.

The evening came and went with nothing of consequence to report, the grand malt, recommended to me by Bert, helping me gain a full night's sleep. But I awoke in the early hours, my mind racing, dreaming of Morgwel.

CHAPTER 8

I packed as much as I could manage for the train, arranging with the hotel manager to retain the remains of my belongings in storage until I could have them collected, paid my bill, leaving a generous tip, including the price of a large malt for barman Bert.

I was to be transported to Paddington in the hotel's own automobile once I had collected Dougy and my cat Willum; the pre-booked tickets would be at the station office. My furry friends were delighted to see me. I paid the bill and then we set off for Paddington.

Everything went swimmingly: a porter helped me with the animals and my small amount of luggage, and soon we were travelling at speed through the English countryside.

On arriving at Exeter there was to be a six-minute stopover, just enough time for Dougy to relieve himself, after which it was on to Penzance, our final destination.

As arranged, the local cab was waiting to ferry me to The Ship where landlord Ted had ensured my room was ready for my occupation. He greeted me like a long-lost friend which was an absolute delight – I was already feeling that Cornwall was home.

As we pulled up to The Ship I had a knot in my stomach. It all looked so familiar, almost like I had lived there, well, forever. Ted was standing at the front door eagerly greeting me; he then proceeded to unload my luggage which he carried to the room.

'Just as before, sir, I hope you will be comfortable. Me missus has put some flowers, like, and fresh lavender, given it a real spruce, and in case you get a bit cold we have laid the fire. Yous can sit there, have a read or look at the harbour. Oh yes, will you be wanting dinner?'

'Mm, yes please, and has Albert been in? I am most anxious to hear some more of his intriguing tales which he left halfway through.'

'Wells, sir, see he's not been in since I think his missus gave him hell for being so late and I knows he has been working all the hours at the hall getting it ready for thee. The Westlakes want it to be pristine for the handover. Even organised my Nancy to get in a team to clean the whole place. I can tell thee, sir, we is so excited. I hope you will be very happy there.'

I remember being touched by the man's enthusiasm: after all, we were barely acquaintances, but it gave me a nice, warm glow inside. Yes indeed, this was home.

My Cornish pasty and chips went down well. Sadly Albert did not make an appearance so I elected to have an early night. My pent-up excitement was overflowing: was I really to be the new owner of such a wonderful abode?

I hardly slept even with a quite heavy meal and several malt whiskies, so at 6.30 I bathed, dressed and took Dougy for an early morning walk along the nearest beach.

It was a perfectly still day, the sun just beginning to burn through an early morning mist, the tide was out and on the turn, the air was filled with the noise of seagulls hunting for food as they dived and weaved on their never-ending quest.

I picked up a small piece of weather-beaten driftwood along the high tideline which I threw as far as my arms could manage. Dougy barked, wagged his tail then proceeded to bring the object back to me. I was completely lost in a dreamlike state. Once again I pondered, was this truly to be my home?

I had walked for some time before the beach turned to pebbles and rocks, then I realised at the top of the cliff looming above was Morgwel. I scanned along the bottom looking for the smugglers' cave but saw nothing.

I checked the time on my Waltham wristwatch that I had purchased just after the outbreak of war. It had seen me through many a battle, its luminous dial a godsend in the trenches. The time was nearing 7.45 and I decided I had ventured far enough. Anyhow, my gammy leg was just starting to play up, and I was suffering with hunger pangs.

Breakfast at The Ship was a lavish affair, or should I best say, large affair: sausages, bacon and eggs, toast, freshly brewed tea, lashings of home-made marmalade: fit for a king was Ted's favourite saying.

Having finished I sat in the bar with another pot of tea, flicking through the local rag, then precisely at 10.30 estate agent Mr James appeared, his face beaming, jangling a set of keys in his right hand.

'Captain, sir, it is done. I received a telephone call not twenty minutes ago to say all legalities are complete and that I can hand you the keys.' He paused, presenting me with a bottle of bubbly hidden behind his back. 'And may I say how delighted I am and be the first to welcome you to this very special part of the world and more importantly a very special home.'

I think at my youngish age I have become far too cynical: my thoughts were that the greedy little man was more pleased with his not small commission. Still, that's how the world works, we have all got what we want: the Westlakes a sale, James some very nice, earnings, and me, well yes, me a wonderful home.

'Why, many thanks, Mr James, you really are too kind.'

'Well, sir, I am to conduct you to your new home where I will officially hand over the keys and well, that's that. Oh and it's been cleaned and polished from head to toe, so to speak, and Mr Albert, the gardener, has worked his magic. In fact, I know he intends to call on you later to discuss his new role with you and the hall.'

I placed the champagne in a small leather holdall that I had packed a few basics in, having previously asked Ted if I could call back in the afternoon or the following morning for the rest of my belongings.

Cat Willum was in his travelling box which I placed carefully on the back seat of Mr James's car, then myself and Dougy clambered aboard. I instructed James to let me and Dougy off a couple of hundred yards from the front entrance.

We quickly reached the hall, Dougy and myself alighting from the car as arranged. James drove off to park, leaving me to stare in awe at my new home. Even my furry friend seemed elated.

'So, boy, this is it, a new chapter in our lives, a new adventure.' Then some 50 yards from the front door I sensed movement from the battlements. I stopped and sure enough, there she was, but this time staring intently out to sea. I hesitated, desperately wanting to call out but James was in the house and I didn't want him questioning me. Dougy barked, causing me to be momentarily distracted, and by the time I looked back she was gone. I shielded my eyes and scanned the whole building, but no, alas, I was alone.

I entered the hallway where James handed me the keys, showing me the spares and others for various parts of the house carefully placed on an oak table, also explaining that the electricity was back on and that he had applied for the telephone to be reconnected, which he believed would take several days.

I thanked him profusely for all his help and proceeded to usher him towards the front door. I needed to be alone to inspect the castle and find her. His last words were for me not to hesitate contacting him on any aspect of the house. I then closed the door firmly.

Willum had begun to meow, probably objecting to the injustice of once more being locked in his temporary box, I let him out, explaining that this was our new home and not to wander too far, laughing to myself as I did so, mumbling, 'As if he can understand.'

I quickly ran, or rather half-limped, to the second sitting room, removing the brick that hid the key to the castle. Opening the lock, I eased open the huge oak door and before me was the first room. I bounded towards the stairs, surprising myself at my newfound agility and pausing every so often to catch my breath.

Then I was there in the open, a fresh wind biting into my reddened face. I was desperate to make contact with who I believed was Anna, but alas I was on my own so I slowly walked around the battlements, stopping at where I had left my sketch.

I can remember vividly stopping dead, catching my breath, rubbing my eyes and looking all around, but no, it was gone: the sketch had vanished. I examined the stones that I had used to secure it, but they were still in place.

Then I noticed from the corner of my eye that the ground had been disturbed and there was an arrow etched into some loose earth pointing towards the edge. My eyes followed the ground until I spotted a small mound, much the same as the previous one where I had discovered her painting. Dougy had disappeared, leaving me quite alone contemplating my next move.

I walked slowly and deliberately towards the clods of earth, having previously discarded my stick. It was as though I had a new lease of life, then I knelt carefully, brushing away the dirt. I could feel some small stones which I pushed aside. I gasped for there was the most perfect picture of the most perfect lady, signed 'Anna', with a kiss.

I studied the picture for several seconds before struggling to stand back up, which without my stick proved to be quite a trauma. I observed that it was damaged on the edges, had faded and was slightly damp. She looked quite young but had a beauty, a presence: I needed to know more.

Then my mind was distracted as I heard the sound of a motor. I peered over the battlements: it was the local food store delivering my initial order. Ted had previously kindly given it to the shopkeeper who was making the pub's biweekly delivery, and made the arrangements, ensuring it was to be at Morgwel that morning.

I called to the driver from the castle, explaining that I would take several minutes to negotiate the stairs and open the door. He replied that he used to deliver the Westlakes' food and would begin to unload at the tradesmen's entrance near to the kitchen.

I eventually reached the rear door and was greeted by a middle-aged-looking man dressed in smart, dark trousers, a plain white shirt and tie with a brown apron; a tweed cap completed the outfit. The name 'Jim Draper, food provisions and fresh vegetables, Penzance, Cornwall' was emblazoned on the canvas covering.

'Good day, Captain, sir, and may I welcome you to Cornwall, more especially to this wonderful manor house and castle. I hope you will be very happy here. My name is Jim Draper, I am the proprietor.'

I liked this man: he appeared pleasant, jolly, kindly-looking and polite yet professional. 'Thank you, Mr Draper. I trust you were able to complete my order?'

'Oh yes, sir, in full and I took the liberty to include some fish from the docks and a nice piece of steak from the butcher. Their calling cards are on the package should you want to order more. Oh and yes, I have set up an account for you which is due the last day of each month, if that is acceptable? And my wife has arranged a couple of bouquets of fresh flowers as a welcoming gift, so to speak. Oh and nearly forgot: Albert sends his apologies but can't make today. He will be in touch as soon as possible: seems his wife is poorly.'

'Why, thank you. I was wondering where he was.' Damn and blast, I thought to myself, another day without getting any nearer to solving any more of the mystery.

We bade each other a good day and then I began to sort out the kitchen and larder. Nancy was to help me six days a week as a part-time housekeeper, but tonight I would be cooking for myself.

CHAPTER 9

'Well, Dougy, looks like it's me and you, old boy. Still, with no one here to spy we can do pretty much what we want and I intend to explore this place, starting as soon as I have packed this lot away.' My faithful companion wagged his tail eagerly as if in recognition of my plan.

I laid out the estate agent's plans of the house on the large kitchen table, poring over them with much scrutiny and deciding to firstly re-explore the internals of the Manor House, then, depending on the time, either the grounds or maybe venture down the steps to the old smugglers' cove and my private beach.

As I was in the kitchen I decided to once more examine the adjacent old servants' quarters. I had been informed that they had been cleaned thoroughly with the largest room fit for usage, in the event that at some future juncture Nancy would be required to stay over.

I had previously sent to a department store in Penzance a list of my requirements, such as furnishings and bedlinen, though for tonight I was happy to use the freshly laundered and made-up sets that had been left behind.

Even though they were spotless and now quite homely, with

the large, heavy drapes removed and windows polished, I still found these rooms spooky. I could not put my finger on why, but as I entered a definite shiver travelled up my spine.

I looked at Dougy. 'Come on, old man. let's be daring time for a real adventure, to the smugglers' cave. Follow me.'

He once again wagged his tail as if in agreement. Maybe he did understand me, I pondered, laughing to myself.

I bounded through the rooms, finally reaching the castle where the stairs descended. 'Right, Dougy, let's check provisions, eh? This could be a long adventure,' I said, tongue in cheek. 'Now let's see, mmm, dog treats and hip flask – yep, all in order.'

On my previous excursion I had decided to leave the entrance unblocked, but as on this occasion I was travelling deeper, I realised a light was needed. I scanned around before spying an old-fashioned oil lamp: all I needed now was some fuel, but curiously as I picked it up I realised it was almost half-full.

Astounded by my good fortune, I fumbled for my matches and lit the wick: immediately the whole area burst into light. This was indeed just what the doctor had ordered.

I called for Dougy to follow and began my descent, soon passing the previous area I had reached: the stairs were slippery in places and quite difficult-going. I noted in the wall face there were occasional cut-out shelves with the remnants of old candles.

I was indeed slightly confused, and if I didn't know better would swear that the passage had been used, perhaps not in immediate recent times, but certainly not that long hence and quite likely in this century.

I also remember the lack of screams, or whatever I had heard previously. Now, as we descended lower there was an eerie silence, apart from the occasional gentle sound of water lapping onto the rocks and sand far below. I was aware the tide was incoming, but an age before it was at full flood, certainly allowing me more than enough time to complete a quick recce.

Dougy negotiated the steps as dogs only do, positively bounding ahead. I brought up the rear, carefully finding my feet but at a steady pace; then in the distance were shafts of light, then sand. I was there, passing a number of potholes and other caves.

It now became obvious why I had not seen it from the beach, as the way it had formed was almost like a wall which looked like part of the cliff, but in fact was hiding the entrance: perfect for smuggling, I thought to myself.

The sun was dipping in and out of clouds, but its warmth was both soothing and calming on my face. There was not a soul to be seen. I selected a large, flat rock that had formed almost like a chair, then sat and took in the view.

Dougy was playing chase with the waves, whilst above seagulls were squawking on their constant hunt for food. The shoreline was awash with seaweed, though I could not see the high tideline, assuming in that case it would be in the cave itself.

'Right, Dougy, old man, come on, I want to explore the cave further,' there looked to be a multitude of different caves and entrances,' looks very interesting.' Like clockwork he wagged his tail in recognition, bounding ahead of me.

I turned, looking at the incoming tide, noting in my opinion there was still plenty of time to go, and at the point it was in I would be safely climbing the stairs to my castle.

Arriving back at the main entrance, I was surprised to note that it was in fact quite low and I had to stoop down to re-enter, also noting that at high tide it would be completely covered with the water penetrating far into the cliff.

I also at last came upon the high tideline in places. 'So which one, eh, old friend? I know. Look, let's follow that tunnel and see where it takes us.'

Just inside the main entrance the cave veered gently to the left. I noted a kind of shaft reaching for the outside, also observing how narrow it was and would not like to get stuck there. I shivered at the thought.

By now, I had lost daylight and the sand gave way to solid rock. I felt myself climbing upwards, stopping to catch my breath, take a snifter, then light a Player's. As I stood motionless I suddenly had a creepy feeling that I was being watched. I swung the lamp from side to side but of course I was quite alone.

Dougy had lost interest and had scampered back to the cave entrance. I knew he would be fine exploring, so I left him to his own devices.

The rock face had now become slippery and it was quite evident that the tide would reach this far, then my mind went blank as a searing pain struck my temple: I had slipped and fallen.

I have no comprehension as to how long I was knocked out but when I eventually came to the water was lapping at my knees and the way back was a mass of foam as the waves battered relentlessly forward.

By some miracle the lamp had not smashed but had become wedged nearby in a small crevice. My head was thumping: I was confused and disorientated. I remember touching my head which was a sticky mess; I had obviously cut myself in the fall.

I just lay there for several minutes trying to clear my mind and ascertain my next move. The water was now lapping at my waist, so I grabbed the lamp and crawled further into the cavern, stopping to gain some breath.

It was as if the water was stalking me, for every foot I crawled it would then splash to my waist. In my befuddled state I knew instinctively I had to climb higher to clear the high tideline.

The roof was now low and curved to my left, then suddenly ahead was the end: a blank wall, the cliff face. I cursed to myself, now quickly coming to as the cold water helped bring me back to my senses.

I held the lamp aloft and could see now that this cave would be filled to the top: there was no option but to go back. At university I could swim nearly two lengths underwater, but now with my wounds, too much alcohol and a somewhat lower level of fitness, I would not be able to do anything like that.

I took a hit from my flask, trying to determine how far I would have to swim to re-enter the main cave and safety. I decided it was the only option. My head now a lot clearer, I reckoned I could hold my breath for about 40 seconds, so I decided to swim for 20, and if I had not reached safety, turn back. Maybe it would be a low tide and I could hold on?

I wedged the lamp as high as possible, the water now just yards away. Taking a quick swig, I began to breathe deeply; to help fill my lungs I stripped down to my underwear, stowing my clothes in the cavern but keeping hold of my trusty lucky flask.

In my mind I counted to three, took one last breath, then plunged into the clear water; it was hard-going fighting the incoming tide but I used the rocks as handles, propelling myself along. I had already reached 10 seconds and there was still no sign of light. 15 seconds: Christ, I would have to make a decision soon.

My hands were hurting as I grabbed at the rocks; some were sharp and pierced my skin, but I continued just ignoring the searing pain, thinking how much I wanted to live.

Then I reached 20. I hesitated but ahead was just the long cave and the furious water. I decided to turn back. I was already struggling: maybe 40 seconds had been ambitious. I was grabbing furiously at the rocks, kicking the water with my feet: my lungs were at bursting point.

I knew in my heart this was it and, as the old cliché goes, my life flashed before me, but curiously the last thing I remember was Anna, the girl in the battlements. I was dizzy, my lungs screaming for air, the pain from my hands, head and inside unbearable. I could feel myself going, then suddenly I was back in the small pocket and safety, albeit for a short time.

The lamp was still glowing, showing me what was probably to be my last resting place, then I made another snap decision: better to die trying to survive. Rather than giving up I would go back into the tunnel and this time not turn back.

Then it happened: I heard the sweetest voice but I was startled and knocked the lamp, plunging me into darkness.

'Captain, I have only just found you. I have already lost in love and could not bear you to be taken by the cruel sea. It is too far to get fully back to the main cave but you can make the small air shaft: trust me, it is narrow but it will save you and this space you're in will fill that, I know.'

'Who are you?' I cried. 'Where are you?'

Then as my eyes adjusted to the gloom I noticed a small beam of light emanating from the top: it was tiny and had been hidden by the light from my lamp. I remembered the long shaft: could I really make it?

I started to panic, calling wildly, 'No, don't go, don't leave me please!'

'I will never leave you, Captain, but please you must go now.'

It was strange for the voice appeared to be directly next to me, then I felt a cold blast of icy air: impossible, I deduced, but it did happen.

I held my breath once more then plunged back into the water. 10, 15, 20 seconds: the point of no return. I battled on, the rocks again tearing at my hands, the tide trying to force me back, but the voice had given me a new strength, a purpose. 30 seconds, 40, my lungs were bursting.

Then a miracle: I glimpsed daylight. I was pretty sure it was the shaft, so close yet still far away. I had hit 50 seconds and would soon pass out… But miraculously I held on, swam into the entrance, then wildly vertically until at last my head cleared the water.

I gasped for air, choking, spluttering, coughing, but as sure as there is a God, I had made safety. It took me a couple of minutes before I could survey the shaft and ascertain my position; I had correctly remembered that the entrance was quite wide but quickly tapered to a very narrow point.

I could see daylight way above me, but it was pure heaven to take in the fresh air. My next problem was the tide which was still incoming. I looked above me, estimating I had maybe another foot before it became too narrow:. The question was how long could I tread water? Then I spotted a small outcrop just enough for me to hold onto.

As the water came on relentlessly I gently drifted higher but managed to secure the handgrip. My next problem was the cold: how long could I stay in these waters? Then suddenly there was a surge and once more I was engulfed, the sea covering my head.

I had thankfully taken a deep breath and managed to hold onto the rock until the wave went down, but if the tide continued to rise I was a gonna for sure.

Then I realised the water was in fact receding. I knew full well the turn took an hour, so I must have got muddled in that what I assumed was the rise was in fact surges through the cave system. I began to shiver more violently as the cold bit.

In my mind I tried to recall the layout of the cave system and soon realised that I was very close to the main entrance. I had to do something before the cold really took over. Calling out to my newfound friend, Anna, I took a deep breath and once more plunged into the sea.

Once again my luck held and I quickly found myself in the main cave entrance, stumbling to get out of the water, then I heard the reassuring bark of Dougy: I had made it. Next job: light a fire, dry off, and try to solve the mystery of that sweet voice.

I positively bounded up the rock stairs with Dougy yapping at my feet, my newfound energy probably from the fact that I was somehow still alive and the wonderful greeting from my faithful dog pleased to see me back in one piece.

CHAPTER 10

I drew a deep bath in the bathroom next to my bedroom, pouring in some crystals. I was still shivering from the cold, but as I immersed myself very quickly the warmth brought me back to some kind of normality.

As I dressed I realised my tummy was rumbling and it had been an age since I had eaten, so next job was to rustle up some supper. My culinary skills are very limited so I selected the steak from the day's delivery and a tasty-looking farmhouse loaf, magic: a wonderful sandwich washed down with a nice bottle of red.

It was still early evening when I finished my meal. With Dougy and Willy also fed I elected to have another tour of my new domain, this time steering clear of the cave, water and stairs, and confining myself to the house, with possibly a last visit to the old castle battlements.

Having piled my dishes and cooking implements into the sink I chose to tour the upstairs bedrooms, beginning with one of two on the third floor. I gingerly pushed open the huge, painted oak door and peered into what appeared a quite gloomy room.

There were a pair of old, black-painted Victorian bedsteads, minus mattresses, some quite elegant furniture, the usual heavy drapes, complemented with a number of rugs that were scattered across the bare timbers.

I shrugged my shoulders – nothing of interest here – but I surmised it would make a nice guest room, as there was a further bathroom in between the two bedrooms, assuming of course anyone would want to visit me.

Now the next room was a mystery for it was locked, the door firmly shut unlike the others; also I cannot explain but I was strangely drawn to it.

As good fortune would have it, or Lady Luck, at the last minute I had selected one of the many bunches of keys just in case of such an eventuality. As I searched for the correct one I inexplicably paused and became quite nervous, of what I have no comprehension.

Eventually I found the correct key and slowly turned the old brass mechanism. The door creaked softly, almost objecting to the intrusion; it was dark and uninviting, the jacquard drapes still drawn, as if the room didn't want to be disturbed.

I fumbled for the light switch which turned on a single bulb hanging from a wire fitment. It was dull and hardly lit the room so I ventured in and pulled the curtains open: from behind I heard a sudden gasp followed by a blast of chilled air, then the door slammed shut.

'Dougy, is that you?' I called. No reply, then I heard a scratching and quickly turned: it was Willy, my cat, who had, unbeknown to me, somehow sneaked in. I breathed a sigh of relief and once more scanned what I could now see of the space and was quite aware of the emptiness, for there was a large double bed, a wardrobe, dressing table and that was it. But towards the end I noticed the wall was covered by a matching curtain which I found odd but was strangely drawn to.

Again for no logical reason I was drawn to this part of the bedroom. On reaching the wall I began to pull open the curtain, then from behind me there was a blood-curdling scream followed by venomous hissing: my cat Willy was spitting, his back arched and teeth showing. Then he ran towards the closed door in a panic.

I immediately dropped the curtain back and rushed over to the terrified animal but he had a wild glint in his eyes, staring at the drape-covered wall and cowering away. I opened the door and he was gone to be replaced by faithful Dougy wagging his tail, happy to be reunited with me.

I leaned forward and stroked him. 'Glad to see you, old man. Don't know what got into Willy. Anyhow come on, let's carry on exploring.' But as I approached the curtain draped across the wall he also cowered away, barking furiously, then turned and scampered off.

I must admit at this point I was somewhat, dare I say, almost scared but nevertheless ventured forth, eventually pulling back the dust-laden cloth to reveal a solid wall covered in a garish wallpaper quite out of keeping.

I stood back, carefully scanning the whole area and trying to fathom what would possess someone to firstly use such a disgusting paper, then cover it with an old curtain. I stood for several minutes going over the area inch by inch, but nothing came to light.

I turned to leave and continue my exploration when I was sure I heard a noise from behind; then from the corner of my eye I spotted a piece of the wallpaper curling upwards, covering what appeared to be some timber.

I leaned forward and tugged at the paper, pulling it up in one large piece, revealing a sheet of timber that appeared to be nailed to a frame. I stopped as again I heard a noise that, well, as daft as it would seem, sounded like a woman crying.

I tugged at more of the paper again, revealing another panel. Leaning forward, I tapped the timber wall and to my surprise it sounded hollow: possibly a secret room, I pondered.

After a considerable time I finally pulled off the last piece: the noise from within had long abated, and Dougy had fallen asleep on a rug. I stepped back, trying to fathom out just what the purpose of the crude woodworking was, and then I spotted what appeared to be the main join in the panels.

It was too small for my fingers so I made my way downstairs to a work cupboard, eventually finding a small toolbox. I selected a chisel, hammer, jemmy and large screwdriver, then returned to the bedroom. Dougy was still asleep and appeared not to have moved.

Selecting the screwdriver, I hammered it behind one of the panels which came away with remarkable ease, leaving enough room for me to force it off the crude frame with the jemmy, which in my opinion had obviously been hastily put together and not very professionally at that.

With one final heave the panel came away to reveal a painted wall which appeared to be part of the original room. I, with much enthusiasm, worked from right to left, tearing at the woodwork, eventually arriving at the centre which revealed a set of hinges emanating from the remaining panel.

I stood back scratching my head again, trying to work out the logic behind the false wall.

Though tiring, I summoned my last bit of strength and ripped the panel off to reveal a door, again obviously part of the original room. On first trying the handle it appeared locked but with a little more effort the mechanism finally turned. I remember hesitating before pulling it slowly open.

To my mind it had been sealed for some time as a large amount of dust, until now not disturbed, floated towards me. I stood back coughing, then it settled and I fumbled inside for a light switch which eventually clicked on.

On first observation it appeared to be a dressing room or study but was windowless and very foreboding, extremely gloomy, quite cold with a slight odour of damp. Then I spotted a WC adjacent to a small desk bureau.

'What a mystery,' I perceived. Again like the adjoining bedroom the single bulb did not throw out much light but I decided anyhow to venture in, quickly checking Dougy was still close just in case I needed to summon help, quite for what I have no idea.

I seated myself adjacent to the bureau, scanning the room with much intensity. All appeared as normal: my mind was pondering any possible scenarios for it to be hidden. I pulled open the desk's drawer to reveal the normal pigeonholes containing the usual assortment of envelopes, blank paper, pens – all the paraphernalia you would expect.

One by one I pulled open the other drawers, most of which appeared to be empty. I even tried to locate any buttons hiding secret compartments often used for hiding correspondence of illicit affairs and such.

Just as I was about to give up my hand brushed against what I considered to be one. I held my breath, trying to work out how it operated, then with a push to the left a drawer popped out, hitting my knees. I gasped, grinning to myself.

Bending down, there was just enough light for me to see it was empty; nevertheless I pushed my hand in just to check and sure enough nothing, then I pushed to the very depths and felt what I could only guess was a photograph, as the paper appeared shiny to my touch.

I eventually managed to grasp the object that seemed to be evading me, then brought it into the light. It was a picture of a very handsome man atop a boat with the ocean in the background: he had a bottle of brandy in one hand, a pistol in the other, and a beaming smile. Scrawled across it was: 'To Anna. With Love, Clifford'.

As ridiculous as it must seem, I actually felt a pang of jealousy for I wanted Anna to be mine. I pocketed the photo and made my way back to the landing, calling for Dougy who dutifully followed.

The evening was drawing in as darkness descended. I decided the main living room too large and selected the smaller, second one adjacent to the castle. The log fire was laid which I proceeded to light with some difficulty but eventually it was ablaze.

Lighting a Player's, I then poured a large malt into a crystal glass sitting back to relax. Both Dougy and Willy were stretched in front of the fire, looking quite at home and at ease with the world.

I quickly finished the glass. Now feeling somewhat groggy, the effects of the wine and now Scotch hitting me, the heat from the fire adding its threepence worth. I groped for another cigarette, instead finding the photograph of Clifford.

I glanced at the man's image before dismissing it onto an adjacent table. I then pulled out the miniature of Anna. I smiled and a warm glow engulfed my stomach; this time it was not the alcohol.

I must have drifted into a light doze as I awoke with a start as the long-case clock (one of three) struck nine o'clock. As my eyes adjusted to the half-light I saw the fire was nearly out so threw on a handful of logs and raked it with the poker.

On the side table next to me was a half-empty bottle of malt, the miniature of Anna plus my cigarettes and the picture of Clifford. An ashtray had a number of dog-ends – 'Must cut down,' I mumbled to myself.

Dougy was still sprawled and I surmised Willy was tucked up in his new wicker basket in the kitchen next to the range. I delved into my jacket pocket until I felt the newest addition to my prized possessions, appertaining to new friend Anna.

I pulled out the faded picture that I had found on the battlements earlier, adding it to the collection on the table. I sat studying her features, then quite suddenly I heard a noise from upstairs, unmistakeably a crash.

Dougy had also heard it and jumped from the comfort of the fire, running towards the stairs barking. I followed immediately without giving it a second thought, then as I bounded up I halted near to the top. Yes, now I could hear scraping as if furniture was being dragged across the floor, coming from what I believed was Anna's old bedroom that I had explored earlier.

I froze, my heart beating as if I had just run the mile in record time. Dougy had also inexplicably stalled but was no longer barking, though he looked rather apprehensive, as if not knowing what he should do.

I covered the remaining steps quietly and with much caution halting outside the bedroom door which was firmly shut. I distinctly remember leaving it open with a doorstop. I could feel a bead of nervous sweat trickling down my forehead before running to my neck.

My hands were shaking, from what I was not sure: fear? Or the possibility I would at last come face to face with the elusive lady who had so captured my heart. Knowing there was no other exit I decided to call out rather than go blindly barging in.

The scraping noise had abated, the only sound now my deep breathing and Dougy panting.

Hesitantly I called out, 'Is someone there? Who are you please? Stay, I just want to talk, don't be frightened.' I laughed to myself: if that wasn't the cat calling the kettle black.

But sadly there was no reply. I gingerly took hold of the brass handle, turning it slowly before pushing the door open. I peered inside, again calling: the lights were on and the drapes now closed, not how I had left the room a few hours prior.

Now I must admit a true fear had overcome me: I was so convinced it was Anna that I had not thought of the possibility it was indeed a cat burglar. I looked around for a weapon but none was to hand.

Calming myself, and deciding the worst would be a scuffle, and after all, I was a trained soldier: what could happen? A few bruises? Then I noticed the door I had discovered earlier was open. I again called out with no reply.

'Come on, Dougy, time to earn your keep. If I am attacked, do your stuff.' But he was frozen to the spot, not barking but emitting a soft growl, his fur standing on end: in fact he began to back away.

I can only surmise it was the alcohol that made me brave as, without thinking, I suddenly leapt forward, opening the door fully: the light was on but the room quite empty. However, then something happened that I cannot fathom. As I stepped in, the air became like a winter's day with a distinct mist. This seemed to rush past me, causing me to shiver at the sudden freezing drop in temperature. I have no logical explanation.

Then suddenly the room returned to normal, desperately disappointed that my Anna was nowhere to be seen. As I scanned the void I noticed a broken oil lamp smashed on the floor; surmising that was possibly the earlier crash, I was about to take my leave when I noticed the dust on the floor had been disturbed and there was a distinct mark scratched in the timber where the bureau had been moved. How I had missed that previously I cannot comprehend.

On closer examination it became apparent that this object had been moved on a regular basis. I examined the floor carefully then spotted a gap in the boards. Pushing the bureau to one side I was surprised at how light it was; then it became obvious these boards had been loosened.

I stooped down, gently prising one up with great ease, then removing the other three one by one. They were smaller than the rest of the room and had obviously been cut down for ease. It appeared to be a secret hiding place, the void disappearing into the side of the wall. Lighting a match to allow me to see into the darkness, it was sadly quite empty.

I was about to move away when something urged me to look again. The room had once more become cold and misty, though on this occasion I was not frightened, in fact quite the opposite. However, I was still unable to see anything untoward.

Then, as if guided by an unknown force, I reached into the depths of the hole, pushing my arm into the wall crevice. I hit metal and, though at quite a stretch, managed to secure the object and brought it back into the room.

It appeared to be an old tobacco tin, quite large in comparison to most and had a European stamp to the front. I elected to open it to discover its contents, and as I did so the cold, misty air seemed to rush past me, the room once more returning to normal.

Inside I discovered a layer of tissue paper which I removed, placing it on the floor. Then I came upon an embroidered silk hanky which I noted immediately had the initials 'A.W.' which was in my mind obviously Anna Westlake. I gasped.

Then again for no logical explanation I reached back into the compartment. This time I felt what appeared to be a wooden object and a bottle. I pulled them back into the room: it looked like the flintlock and brandy that Clifford was holding in the newly found picture.

I have to admit again I was a little jealous as it became clear there was probably some sort of liaison between the pair, but I quickly shrugged the notion off, trying to fathom why these objects were hidden in such a surreptitious manner.

On returning to the fire I poured myself a large malt, placing the pistol and brandy to one side but clasping hold of the hanky. The flames were again beginning to dim, then as I leaned forward noted some ash appeared to have fallen onto the timber floor away from the grate.

I leaned forward, selecting the old Georgian brush then noticed there were some words drawn in the ash. I blinked, doing a double take: it was not clear and somewhat difficult to read but sure enough: 'To My Brave Captain. With love, Anna', then in brackets, 'The Handkerchief is a gift from me'.

I gasped, falling back into my chair before leaning forward to read the words again. Then from nowhere Dougy came bounding in, demolishing the ash. I leaned back searching for my glass of whisky, taking down a huge gulp. I was indeed confused and mystified.

I remember sitting there, the fire crackling, Dougy fast asleep, letting out the occasional whimper. I chain-smoked and very nearly finished the bottle of malt. My eyes were heavy: I would soon drop off. Then the clock struck 11.00. I somehow managed to get myself together and retired to the master bedroom.

I stumbled into my bathroom and had a quick wash then stripped off, tugging on my pyjamas. I would not say I was drunk but certainly let's say very relaxed. I clambered between the crisp sheets with the mountainous eiderdown. Dougy sat looking, his big, brown eyes pleading.

'Come on, boy, but that's your end.' I pointed to the other side of the bed: he knew the drill, leapt up, then snuggled down, now quite content.

CHAPTER 11

My sleep as normal was restless and broken. I had long stopped taking some pills the quack had prescribed, never sure what their purpose was only that if I drank I often felt quite nauseous, then all went blank as I eventually dozed off.

But our bliss was not to be for long as a couple of hours later I heard another crash followed by banging but this time in the old nursery just along the corridor from my room. I swear also I heard a child whimpering.

The effects of the alcohol had begun to wear off, though my eyes were blurry and I was somewhat befuddled. I remember securing my thick, checked dressing gown and tying the cord tight, then called Dougy to follow.

Again mysteriously the door was firmly shut. I stood outside. The banging had stopped but I could hear a strange creaking noise. 'Hello, who is there please?' I cried out but again no reply.

Taking a deep breath I pushed open the door. It was dark and gloomy. I reached for the light switch and stopped dead for there in the centre of the room the rocking horse was going at full strength up and down at some considerable speed as if a child was indeed playing with the toy.

I searched the room but of course there was no one to be seen. The drapes were wide open and I could see the shutter had been opened, I surmised by the wind, though I must confess I found the whole episode most disconcerting.

I gently stopped the horse dead before securing the shutters: how on earth had they become dislodged? There was not even a gentle breeze tonight, let alone a gust of wind to open them. Anyhow, I know I had previously secured them firmly.

'Blimey, Dougy, what a first night, eh, old boy? Never a dull moment. I think I need a drink.'

We walked together back down the stairs, the last embers of the fire still glowing though just enough to kick-start it again. Soon the flames were blazing. I lit a Player's and poured some malt: too wide awake for sleep, at least for the present.

The next few minutes I have no logical reasoning but was glad that what took place did so.

My bottle was now empty so I ventured to the kitchen, opening the larder where my more than ample supply was stored. I selected a Glenfiddich, at the same time grasping a fresh packet of Players.

Dougy had remained by the fire, secured a treat, thank God for him, I thought always loyal and by my side giving me that feeling of protection.

I returned to the living room which was dimly lit only by the fire and a single floor lamp beside another leather chair. Then as I sat I felt cold: the mist had returned, then I realised I was not alone for there as true as I am Captain Williamson was Anna sitting, smiling directly at me.

Rudely my jaw dropped open and I found myself staring at her beauty. 'I am so sorry, Madam, but it is indeed an honour to at last meet. I presume you are Anna.' I wispered not really knowing what to say.

There was no reply; she simply smiled. I remember distinctly I found it hard to focus on her as ridiculous at it would seem. If I didn't know better she appeared almost, well, translucent for want of a better expression. She also had a strange glow that I at first deduced was the reflection from the fire, but no, this was different.

I sat mesmerised. She smiled directly at me. 'Please, Anna, say something. Why do you keep disappearing? Please don't go, just talk. I have longed for your company since I first caught sight of you on the castle battlements.'

But she just sat there smiling. I turned for my malt and when I looked back the chair was empty and the room quite warm. I was completely dumbfounded at was happening to me or indeed what mystery this house was hiding.

I lit another Player's, gulped greedily at my malt, then simply sat there agog at what had just occurred, then suddenly I felt a searing pain in my right hand as the cigarette had smouldered down, burning my finger: indeed it brought me to with a jolt.

For several minutes, maybe longer, I sat mesmerised, staring at the empty chair, taking at least two or more hits of whisky. Was I going mad? Was I imagining things? The doc had said there would be flashbacks to the war, but no, this was different. Then I reached for the pictures and hanky: 'No, I have tangible proof,' I mumbled to myself.

I leaned forward, throwing several logs onto the fire, then settled back. I was far too comfortable to move so I simply pulled on one of the sofa's throws: that was as good as a blanket, then everything went blank as I fell asleep.

CHAPTER 12

The next I recall was the mighty brass knocker on my front door booming out its message that I had a visitor. I looked access at the long-case: it was 8.30. I quickly composed myself to the best of my ability then trotted off to the main entrance.

As I pulled open the door my blurry eyes focused on a young boy, probably about 14, dressed in short, grey trousers, a plain shirt and a pullover that was two sizes too big, plus old leather shoes that also looked larger than his feet.

'Morning, sir, sorry to bother you, like, but I have two messages and I wanted to introduce myself.'

I yawned, scratching my morning stubble. 'Yes, young man, fire away.'

'Well, sir, the messages first with apologies, but Miss Nancy fell in the pub cellar last night and twisted her ankle. She says she can definitely be in tomorrow and Mr Albert has taken his wife to hospital but is pretty sure he will also be in tomorrow.'

'Why, thank you, kindly young man.' I fumbled for a couple of pennies.

'And now's me, sir, I am Dodger. Well's that's not me real name, that's Charlie, but that's what everyone calls me, Dodger at your service.' He bowed graciously, bringing a smile to my face at his obvious intent on what he perceived as a proper greeting. 'Now's there is nothing I can't turn my hand to, so if you needs you boots polished, an errand run, shopping, anything I'm is your man, and very cheap too, so don't forget, just leave a message at the pub or post office.'

I leaned forward, handing him the money. 'Thank you, Dodger, here are a couple of pennies for your trouble and I will certainly be needing some help.'

'Thanks thee kindly, sir but that won't be necessary, only to pleased to bring you the message and make your acquaintance.'

'Please, I insist, keep the money. Oh yes, one thing: could you arrange for a cab to pick me up here at about 10.30? I need to visit Penzance.'

He tipped his cap. 'Think it's done already, sir.' Then he turned, running down my drive, looking at the money I had given him with great delight.

I returned to the kitchen. 'Well, Dougy, old man, looks like all my plans for today have been scuppered. I was hoping to have a nice, long chat with Nancy and Albert and learn some more history. Oh well, never mind. Come on, I need to get ready: have a little business in town I can do instead.'

I made a cup of tea and breakfasted on two boiled eggs and the remains of last night's farmhouse loaf then ran a bath, shaved, greased my hair, selected a nice, crisp, fresh uniform and was ready.

I eventually decided to leave Dougy at home as I intended to call in at the bank and main post office, and thought it inappropriate and unprofessional for him to tag along. Bang on 10.30 I heard the sound of an automobile engine: it was the cab, dead on time.

As I stepped from the door I realised it was the cheery man who had chauffeured me around previously, though I confess I had forgotten his name. He tipped his cap then held open one of the back doors.

'And how are you today, sir? May I greet you to a little piece of Heaven and hope you will be truly happy in that wonderful manor house.'

I thanked him for his kindness then settled back for the ride to Penzance. Little was said, barring an exchange of a few pleasantries and polite conversation, though I managed to secure his services for the whole morning and possibly part of the afternoon.

As agreed, he pulled over a short distance from the main town. After explaining that it was a lovely walk past the harbour and into the centre he showed me the spot he would wait and bade me a good day.

I easily found the bank and arranged for a cheque account from my main branch in London: the manager was a very amiable chap. Next on my list was the post office. I presented them with my telephone number and instructed the manager that if there were any parcels or correspondence he would please be so kind as to phone me, though at present I explained I was still not connected.

As I left the main town I cannot explain in any logical sense what happened next. I was feeling tired and wanted to get back home, but for a strange reason was drawn down one of the many windy side streets: it was an area quite off the beaten track.

I could still hear the annoying squawk of the seagulls as they chased the latest fishing boats into nearby Newlyn harbour, but the lane itself was quite deserted. Then to my astonishment I came upon a tiny shop: 'Madam Rose: Your Fortune Told'.

I was for some reason drawn to the premises. The outside was painted in a garish yellow, the windows were slightly darkened with a white polish of sorts through which I observed a large crystal ball and other paraphernalia, I surmised, relating to the telling of fortunes.

I hesitated but then pushed open the door: a bell rang somewhere in the depths of the building. I stood for a few seconds before an elderly, wily-looking woman appeared. She was dressed in a flowery frock with an old cardigan thrown over her shoulders. I have no logic but she gave me the creeps.

'Ar, it's you. Thee at last found me, haves thee?'

I was quite taken aback. 'I am sorry, madam, but have we met?'

She smiled, revealing several missing teeth, then to my surprise she took out an old clay pipe. 'Sits yourself down there, good, sir, if yous please.'

I seated myself behind the round table housing a small crystal ball and an old china teapot, a single cup and a jar of tea leaves: there were also various packs of cards, beads and an assortment of jars.

'No, sir, thee don't know me but I do thee. I have been waiting patiently for you to call on me.'

I must confess at this juncture I felt quite uncomfortable

but resisted the notion to walk out, my curiosity getting the better of common sense.

'Pray continue, madam, but you have me at a disadvantage for I do not know you.'

She grinned. 'Didn't thee read the sign, sir? Why, I am Madam Rose.' She let out a loud cackle that I must confess was quite disturbing.

'If you persist in this manner I will be forced to leave,' I blurted out without any thought.

'Stay seated, sir, and I apologise. It's me way, see, and all this.' She pointed to the various artefacts such as crystal balls, teacups and the like. 'Well, it's for those who come holidaying, but suffice to say I have a genuine gift and to be clear I wants nothing from thee for what I am about to offer.'

I was indeed mystified and elected to stay.

'Can I get thee a cup of tea?'

I remember raising my eyebrows with a grin. 'What, so you can read my fortune?' I questioned.

'No, sir, in case you are thirsty. Thems things, as I told you, are for the visitors.'

I could see she had a sense of humour, but also a serious side indeed which I was to witness later in the day. I declined the offer of a drink. 'So, madam, pray, how do you know of me?'

'Well, to be clear, sir, I don't know your name or much else but I had a premonition that a young Army officer would visit me and that I would be able to assist in a quest that I believe appertains to a house that thee have recently moved into.'

I began to feel rather uncomfortable and fidgeted nervously. Was she genuine or just good at reading people and drawing them in? But then I had not really said much, though dressed in my uniform it was quite obvious I was a military man.

'Well, yes, it is true that I have recently moved here and occupied a wonderful old manor house, but how could you possibly know?' I hesitated and needed to word my next conversation carefully. 'And suffice to say, er, mm, how can I put it? There have been some strange occurrences.'

'Mm, I thought as much, and were you inexplicably drawn here to me.'

'Yes, madam.'

'Now please listen, I am not here to trick thee or gain cash before, well, let's say needs must, and I needed to make a living, so I opened this shop. I was very well known in spiritual circles and much respected.' She paused, looking directly at me. 'Now then, young sir, let's be clear: I don't want to know anything that has been happening apart from is your property far?'

'No, madam, not that a distance: it's Morgwel Hall.'

'Mm, vaguely rings a bell, though I am not very well travelled. Tend to stay in Penzance since I moved here, so do you require me to visit? As I said, no fee. I can tell you are somewhat troubled.'

'Well, yes, madam, perhaps clear the air once and for all, so to speak.'

'Fine. Please write down your address: I will visit this evening. I have no means of transport but will happily get the bus.'

I fumbled in my pocket for some notes. 'Here, madam, please take a cab on me – least I can do.'

'Mm, well, thanks thee kindly: never had the pleasure until now. I will see you at 8.00 on the dot.'

The doorbell sounded as two women in their twenties entered the shop giggling and whispering. I stood, saluted Madam Rose, then took my leave.

On the way home I took a slight detour to The Ship and paid off the taxi, deciding to take a leisurely stroll home. Landlord Ted greeted me like a long-lost friend, calling Nancy to fetch tea and cakes.

As the timid girl made her appearance with the tray of delights she whispered an apology and that she would for sure be working the following day. Then she disappeared. I thoroughly enjoyed my tea and cakes and decided to stay for an early supper rather than cook for myself again.

Sadly my gardener Albert did not make an appearance, but Ted assured me that he, too, would be up at the manor the following day to work. My pasty and chips were a pure delight, so having feasted well I paid my dues and made my way back to the hall.

Arriving back home, Dougy greeted me as though I had been gone for weeks. Even Willy made an appearance, sidling up my leg and purring to his heart's content. The house felt different as though it was at last at peace with itself: maybe my imagination had been running wild.

CHAPTER 13

It was nearly 7.30 and for no reason I was becoming slightly apprehensive of my impending visit from Madam Rose. I readied the kettle expecting she would enjoy a cup of tea, then took a small snifter from my flask, intending to keep a clear head.

Just before 8.00 I heard the crunch of tyres on the gravel drive and made my way to the front door. It was the local taxi firm from Penzance with my visitor Madam Rose. I sauntered over to the driver and bade him to wait at The Ship to return Rose later that evening.

He happily agreed. I invited my new acquaintance into my home then suddenly she stopped dead in her tracks and peered straight at the old battlements. 'Mm, young man, I can see this is going to be an interesting visit – yes, very interesting,' she mumbled.

I brought her through into the kitchen, supposing she would like to be refreshed with a cup of tea which she politely declined, but not before leaving some herbal leaves that she would partake later. She took out her clay pipe which she duly lit, taking several puffs before it went out of its own accord.

'So, Captain, as I said earlier, please do not volunteer any information, just please answer the occasional question.' She paused, taking in the surroundings. 'So I need a tour of the house please, and would like to take in the old castle at some point.' She then stopped and appeared to be listening intently. I confess there was not a sound, then she shivered, a knowing grin enveloping her ruddy face.

'Please, where does that hallway lead to? Are there any rooms?'

She pointed towards the old servants' quarters where Nancy's friend and mother were stationed.

'Why, yes, Madam Rose. I suppose as we are close this is as good a place to begin as any.'

She followed me several steps behind, looking all around and occasionally stopping – for what reason I could not fathom. Then we came to the mother's room which she entered and gave a quick look around, shaking her head in a negative way. 'Mm, much sadness here, my boy, much sadness. And not that many years past either.'

We then entered the grandest of the three rooms, with the double bedstead. She stopped abruptly not three steps in, and shivered and gasped. 'Much evil doings in here, young Captain. I can feel it: violence, screams, a tormented, twisted soul in search of atonement. 'Don't worry, I am here to help,' whispered Rose in a kindly voice.

The suddenly the room became like ice. The door slammed, I swear I heard a scream, and the window shutters smashed against the wall.

'Be gone with you, I have no time for thee!' screamed Rose, then the room appeared to return to some normality. I was indeed quite disturbed but at the same time much intrigued. Common sense said stop, but I could not help myself: I wanted to know more.

She was about to leave when she again abruptly halted. The room once more became cold, the atmosphere strange, yet calmer than previously. 'Mm, now then, young Captain, I am sensing great sadness. The violence has gone but this is, well, quite upsetting. I don't know what happened in this room but I can tell thee it was of great wrongdoings, violence, lust, all tinged with sadness.'

I saw her scanning the room intently, moving towards the bed and examining the wall. I am sure she didn't comprehend but I did notice that the end wall was out of sequence with the building, almost as if there was another false chamber hidden. Indeed, out of character there was an old tapestry from ceiling to floor that I had not perceived on my last visit.

Then Madam Rose lit her pipe again, took several puffs and called, 'I have seen enough here. So please, I am drawn to upstairs. Maybe a nursery. Yes, that's it, a nursery. Mm, wait. Yes, I can see it clearly: a rocking horse is in the centre of the room.'

It was my turn to shiver. In fact, I am sure I turned quite white at her statement. Yes, a house like this would have a nursery and possibly a rocking horse, but I could see she knew for sure. Then as we reached the landing, she walked straight to the nursery door, not a moment's hesitation.

'This is it, I presume, Captain?'

I nodded.

She turned the handle to no avail. 'It's locked, Captain. Do you have the key?'

'No Madam, it should not be. Why, only last night I was here.' I tried it and much to my confusion it was firmly shut, the Chubb lock engaged, the handle turning, but alas not opening.

I ran as fast as my legs would carry me, returning with one of the many sets of keys. This set was, I knew full well, for the upstairs. One by one I tried each, then success as the lock finally opened.

She slowly pushed the door and I was astonished at what my eyes beheld. The rocking horse was moving so violently that I thought at any moment it would lift off or crash to the floorboards. There appeared to be a swirling mist; indeed, I rubbed my eyes and took a second look.

Madam Rose entered, beckoning me to follow; she lit her pipe. 'Mm, nothing evil here, Captain, but I sense something, yes, a real tragedy. Indeed, immense sadness in this place, yes, sadness. There is indeed a restless youngster.' Then it all stopped: I was really unnerved.

She moved slowly towards the rocking horse, calmly slowing it to a stop. The room felt like ice, then I heard a child's voice giggling, laughing. I looked around but of course there was no one to be seen. I must confess I could put no logical interpretation on these events and normally would have run a mile, but Madam Rose seemed to have an air about her that made one feel quite safe.

Then the giggling ceased. I heard a cry and what would appear to be a crash or bump, then a deadly silence. Madam

Rose lit her pipe, sitting in an old nursing chair. 'I sense a life gone before its time here, Captain. Yes, as I said, an immense tragedy took place in this room and I must say not that many years past.'

She sat for several minutes puffing at the clay pipe, the smoke drifting aimlessly towards the celling. Then she changed over to a rocking chair and swayed gently at an almost static rhythm, the cold and mist gradually dispersing.

Then as I approached her, Madam Rose's eyes appeared fixated: she was staring blankly ahead. As I moved nearer it became apparent she was almost in a trance-like state. Indeed, I waved my hand to her face and she did not even blink.

Then I must confess I became quite perplexed for, as she opened her mouth and a strange, gruff voice was emitted, she appeared to be talking in a peculiar language that I had never come across. I then became quite frightened, calling her name but to no avail.

Her voice was becoming louder, her breathing laboured, yet still she remained in a trance-like state. Her eyes now appeared dead and if she was not still speaking and gasping that would have been my conclusion.

There was a deadlock which lasted several minutes during which I considered that I had still not really learned any substantial facts, though of course it was now clear that there had been some immense happenings.

I was quite at my wit's end what to do, then suddenly without warning she came to, beamed me a smile and stood from the chair.

At this point I realised that poor Dougy was nowhere to be seen, which was probably the best option for him under these very bizarre circumstances, and was hopefully snuggled in his new bed.

'I am sorry, Captain, but I should have warned you that sometimes my body is taken over by those on the other side wishing to send a message or contact the living. It is an age since that has happened there are some very powerful forces at work here.'

'Why Madam, I was indeed quite perplexed as to what action I should take. Please tell me what I should do if that happens again.'

'Oh nothing, just leave me be and under no circumstances try to bring me round. I'll be back like a bad penny, don't you worry about that.' She paused. 'Now I am most strongly drawn to the battlements: please lead the way.'

As we left the second sitting room and entered the original castle she again came to a halt, walking towards the stairway leading down to the cove. 'My word, Captain, it's here also, but this time I fear many souls perished in those black depths. Pray tell me, I assume this leads to the sea. I feel at some point there was illicit business, probably smuggling, but an immense tragedy where many lost their lives.' She paused, but before I could answer, continued. 'Anyhow it's the battlements I am most in need of seeing.'

I must say considering her age and size Madam Rose took the steps as a young athlete; indeed, with my gammy leg and lack of fitness I struggled to keep up, then suddenly like a breath of fresh air we were at the top and outside.

I noticed her breathing had become laboured and she stood for several minutes gaining her breath back, but at the same time scanning the area, her eyes becoming fixed on the brambles and the clod of earth where I had dug up the metal box.

After several minutes Madam Rose strode across the castle top, standing by the brambles, then walked and stared out to sea. She turned to me.

'This place has a special meaning for thee, young Captain. I can see there have been some mystifying events taking place since you arrived here.'

'Why, yes, in fact.' But annoyingly before I could tell her she raised a hand commanding me not to pass on any facts.

'There is a lady that spent many an hour gazing out to sea. I have no idea why but she was probably looking for someone. Then I can see her dancing, then much sadness. Does the name Anna have a meaning for thee?'

To this I was most disturbed and must have shown my fear, for she told me not to be frightened and that in fact all was good and all would turn out better than my wildest dreams. 'Why, yes, it does.'

'Mm, well, young man, I think your heart has been lost to this person. Does this saying mean anything?' Then she proceeded. I almost fainted and turned deathly white as she recited, 'A love so strong it transcends even death.'

Her next actions worried me immensely for she collapsed in a heap; I rushed to help her. 'I am sorry, young man, it is many years since I have felt so much, but I now feel it is time for me to leave. I have done my job, Captain. I know you have both loved and lost but go with your heart. Think carefully what she wrote to you.'

'Yes, but Madam, please, I have not had a conversation. She comes and goes, appears then disappears. Can you do nothing more?'

She grinned a knowing look. 'You are an intelligent man, Captain, you work it out. Don't think too deeply and one day soon you will know what to do. Meanwhile, during the time we have been here I can feel Anna's presence growing even stronger by the minute. Now I must be off.' She paused. 'I will say this, though. Her soul is troubled but since your arrival has gained a new purpose and has moved on from whatever tragedy befell her.'

She began the descent before me, then I had for no reason an urge to turn, and as I did so saw the beautiful Anna. She was not as translucent; in fact, I felt I could reach out and touch her. I called her name which was returned with a smile.

Then on the wind the words repeated: 'A love so strong...' I called out, 'Anna, my love!' She again smiled and was gone. I decided not to share these events with Rose.

The past couple of hours had left me extremely confused and I desperately wanted Rose to stay: the time had flown by. As we stood by the front door awaiting the return of the cab I thanked her profusely and asked if there was anything she needed, to which she simply shrugged her shoulders.

The taxi arrived. I circled the fountain, walking forward to open the rear door then turned to beckon her in, and to my astonishment she was no longer there. I called her name, indeed made a brief search of the front garden and hall, but she was gone, simply vanished into thin air.

I was somewhat mystified but was fast becoming used to the strange occurrences appertaining to my new home. I smiled at the driver, feigning some ridiculous excuse and paid him off, then returned to the house to be greeted by Dougy wagging his tail and beaming those brown eyes.

CHAPTER 14

'Well, Dougy, old man, what about that for an entertaining evening? God, I need a large drink and cigarette.'

I poured myself a malt before settling in living room two. The open fire was still smouldering – just – with the sweet smell of apple logs floating gently through the air, making the atmosphere feel quite calming.

I quickly finished my drink, pouring another and selecting a Player's, then I began to try and make sense of my visit from Madam Rose. She had told me a great deal but of course there were still many parts to the puzzle unsolved.

I ventured back into the kitchen and saw that Rose had left her herbal tea. I opened the jar and was pleasantly surprised at the appealing odour and ventured to brew myself a cup. I poured boiling water onto the assortment of leaves in a steel pot, leaving them to settle for about five minutes.

Stupidly I forgot a strainer and an amount of leaves entered my cup, though conveniently settling at the bottom. I took a quick slurp and must say it was most agreeable. Taking that and a fresh bottle of Glenlivet, I once more settled in the sitting room.

My mind again pondered the events. I recalled what she had said, that I was a clever man and should work things out and I would know what was to be done. Well, at this juncture I can say I was quite confused.

I had finished my tea and was lighting another Player's when my eyes drifted across the room: there again was the lovely Anna sitting on an armchair adjacent to the door. I immediately smiled, then suggested she come and sit with me.

She simply smiled but her demeanour appeared somewhat different: on this occasion she seemed more, for want of a better expression, solid and there was no cold, icy feel to the air.

'Hello, Anna, please stay a little longer and engage in a conversation with me,' I begged.

She smiled. I then noticed her lips moving as though she was trying to speak, but alas, there was no diction. Then to my astonishment she began to cry, the tears rolling down her cheeks. Foolishly I turned for a hanky, and when I looked back she had gone. I was mystified as I am sure I had heard her voice in the cave and other places.

I hurried to the seat and looked in startled amazement for, sure enough, there on the armrest and floor were the remains of her tears. I then realised that Dougy was seated by the fire and had not moved. What on earth was happening?

Then, for a reason I cannot qualify, my mind drifted back to the Western Front. I had seen many young men perish, thousands, but some, I am sure, came back and saluted to pay their final respects and goodbye. The shrink said it was all part of the symptoms of shell-shock, but I knew better.

Having enjoyed the tea somewhat I made my way back into the kitchen, whereupon my eyes met an inexplicable sight, for the teapot had been overturned and the contents scattered about the table. I searched for a cloth but as I approached realised there were words drawn in the leaves.

'Join Me. Anna x'

I was completely taken aback and immediately wished Madam Rose was still with me, then of course I realised leaving the tea was intentional, then all became clear and I began to formulate a plan for my future but still needed the blanks in the story filled in, I would seek Nancy's input when she arrived first thing in the morning.

I retired to my rooms as excited as possible for simply an age: at long last I was beginning to understand more and started forming a new road to travel on.

The following morning I awoke early, feeling a new determination within. I would speak with Nancy the moment she arrived for work and ask her to continue with her version of the facts appertaining to Morgwel Hall.

I was in the kitchen when Nancy appeared, letting herself in the rear tradesmen's door. I greeted her with a smile, offering a cup of tea and quickly explaining that before she began the day's duties I needed to hear the completion of her story.

She made her apologies for not attending to me the past couple of days, which I dismissed, eager for the continuing mystery to unravel. At this point I decided not to share my meetings with Madam Rose and her findings.

It was a pleasant enough day so we sat outside adjacent to one of the ponds, she on a travel blanket, myself on an old bench that I noted was in need of some TLC.

'So, Captain, sir, as I recall I had got to the point where my best friend Elsa had started to become withdrawn, sometimes failing to turn up for one of our adventures. She became morose and sad; indeed, we hardly had a conversation which was at odds, for we shared all with each other.'

'Then as I recall telling you, one day she arrived with a black eye and some bruising. She looked in a state but on this occasion did confide in me. So apparently for some time she had been flirting with the Westlakes' son, Master Charles, Now he was a handsome man, but a bit of a loner, full of mystery, very deep. It was hard to fathom him, though he did like the ladies and a good time, and was often drunk at The Ship. I recall he didn't really have any friends. So apparently one day they had the house to themselves, Albert was not in, the Westlakes were in Exeter with daughter Mistress Anna, and my mother also had a day off. The flirting began in the morning with Elsa playing hard to get, then Master Charles began drinking and flew into a rage when his advances were halted. You see, she enjoyed the attention but didn't want to take things further.'

Poor Nancy blushed as she spoke. 'Then he lashed out at her, causing a black eye and some bruising. She somehow was able to lock herself in a room until he drank himself silly and passed out. That evening she managed to evade contact with the family and the following day we met. I can tell you I was fuming and wanted to report him, but as Elsa pointed out she and her mother would have been dismissed instantly, be without jobs, homeless and with no references. She told me she could look after herself, gave me a hug, then went back to the hall.'

'My goodness, Nancy, are you fine with reciting this to me?'

'Why, yes, sir, though of course it does sadden me somewhat. Oh and sorry, I was to give you this letter from the bank in Penzance. Apparently there was an error yesterday and they require you to visit them at your convenience sometime this morning.'

I clasped the letter, stuffing it without interest into my jacket pocket on this occasion, intent on Nancy at last concluding the story.

'Then one evening there was a tapping on the window of my bedroom. It was Elsa: she told me that things were a lot better. I was not to worry but that she would not be rendezvousing with me on her day off as the summer season was approaching and Mr and Mrs Westlake had a full diary of entertaining and needed her to work. But I tell thee, sir, it is true enough often through the summer she would work without a break, but for some reason on this occasion I was not convinced. We had no contact until some four months on I had to visit the hall with some of my mum's Cornish pasties. All a bit odd, I mean them being proper posh and the like. Anyhow I went round the back, like today, and nearly dropped on the spot for there was Elsa, a bump as big as you like, pregnant.'

She paused, gathering her composure, a single tear appearing on her cheek. 'Now then, Captain, sir, that was to be the last time we ever spoke. She went away with her mother, returning once the baby was born. Then the Westlakes put out the story that the newborn baby boy was the Lady of the hall, Madam Evelyn's, for they had cancelled all engagements to hide the fact she was not with child and rented a house where they were not known.' She stopped, once more wiping a further tear.

'Goodness me, Miss Nancy, that is quite a story. Are you sure you are able to continue?'

'Oh yes, for there is much more. Now the intention was for Elsa and her mother to take up residence on a trial basis, but Master Charles once more began his old ways, so the family, to avoid scandal, sent him away to the Army, do his duty on the Western Front. I understand he was killed early on at the Battle of the Marne – well, that was the story put about. Mrs Westlake took to the baby as though it was her own and found a new lease of life, at my friend's expense who could only watch the child from afar. Then one day they were summoned to the master who then paid them off and were told never to darken the hall again, or in fact, Cornwall – well, that's the story, somewhat shortened for you, but I was never convinced. You see, Elsa was strong-willed and there was no way she would not have somehow contacted me.'

'So what do you think happened?' I enquired.

'Well, there was a rumour from Albert. You see, he had a soft spot for Miss Anna.'

At the mention of her name I felt myself melt. Indeed as fascinating as this story was, I wanted desperately to hear her story.

'I don't mean romantically, more like a daughter. He felt sorry for her and she often confided in him. Well, apparently the son, Master Charles had come across a hidden secret room.

I think maybe they were murdered or imprisoned.'

I raised my eyebrows, also remembering the wall in the servants' room that I had discovered yesterday and the interest Madam Rose had in it.

'Of course I have no facts to back my thoughts up. It's just well after all these years I can't believe she didn't try and of course the tragedy with baby Harold.'

'What, there's more?' I exclaimed, pausing. 'I beg your pardon, please continue. Enlighten me as to the child's fate.'

'Why yes, sir, Captain, there is more. Well, you see, young Harold continued to grow and gain strength. He was a bonny thing on the odd occasion I saw him. The Westlakes had new staff and very rarely called on me. Perhaps if there was a big event or they had large numbers of guests staying over. Oh and yes, there was a nanny. Didn't really like her, very strict, bit like a matron. Anyhow, you can imagine the nursery had every modern toy but Harold's favourite was the rocking horse: apparently he would spend hours playing with the thing then one day he was rocking the thing at his usual mad pace and the thing toppled. He was thrown, hit his head and died from his injuries sometime later. The local doctor was called but it was too late: the little one had perished.'

At the revelation of the child's death on the rocking horse I felt quite ill, for as you know I have witnessed at first-hand the thing swaying at a pace, and indeed have heard bumps. It was all now falling into place. I looked across at Nancy contemplating the unfolding tragedy, but at last pleased that I was managing to piece together some of the mystery.

'So that's it really, sir. As you know they packed up and left.'

'So what about Anna?'

'Wells, sir, best speak to Albert. My knowledge is patchy but he can tell you the full story and sir, I have me duties and look it's 11.00, you need to get to the bank.'

I was disappointed her prose had ceased but agreed that I needed to busy myself if I was to sort out any problems with the bank. I walked to The Ship where, as luck would have it, the local taxi often parked, and he drove me into Penzance.

I finished my business, which much annoyed me as it was some young clerk who had made a mistake and not I, but then decided to visit my friend Madam Rose and pass on my new knowledge regarding the hall.

I walked past the docks coming upon Fish Street which, as I recall, was where her shop was located, but imagine my surprise when I approached the building. It was indeed boarded with a 'For Sale' sign. I looked again: it was definitely her abode as I could see remains of the garish yellow paint flaking off.

I ventured into the neighbouring store, a haberdasher's, to be told the strangest story. The shop had indeed been empty for the past few years and no one would take it on because, so the rumour goes, the previous occupant is haunting it. I can tell thee I was dumbfounded.

I thanked the proprietor for her help then set off for home, anxious to utilise what time was left in the day by hearing the remains of my gardener's story. I arrived back at Morgwel, quickly paying off the cab and began searching for Albert.

CHAPTER 15

I eventually came across him in one of the glasshouses. 'So, Albert, are you game for continuing the story of my new home?'

'Why, hello, Captain. Of course, if that is what you wish.'

I suggested we made our way back to the house, brew a nice cup of tea and he enlighten me. I was indeed on fire and could hardly contain myself: at last the final piece of the puzzle was to be put in place.

'I suppose Miss Nancy has told you most, Captain?'

'Well, yes, but said she would leave Anna's story to you as she was not as well acquainted with all the facts. But I heard the sad story of the baby and all the intrigue with Master Charles, then the servants missing. Rum affair if you ask me.'

'Yes, Captain, sir, no one ever really did get to the bottom of it all and I suppose now we never will, though of course the baby's death was tragic and I am sure Master Charles died on the Western Front. But as for Miss Elsa and her mother I am sad to say we will probably never know what fate befell them.'

Albert paused briefly as if gathering his thoughts before continuing. 'Right, then, sir, on to Miss Anna. Well, there's a sad story, to be sure. You know, I sort of took her under my wing, so to speak. I always felt somewhat sorry for her. From a young age she loved the outdoors and assisting me in me chores in the garden. A kind of friendship developed. She was a lovely-looking lady with a truly bubbly personality and so bright, but she always lived under the shadow of her big brother, Master Charles, him being the older and of course a male. Well, that is until he disgraced himself and the like. Sorry to be a burden, Captain, but could I please have a couple of sugars in me tea? Gives me energy when I am doing me work, like.'

I passed the bowl over then lit a Player's, making myself comfortable on one of the kitchen's country Windsor chairs, also sneaking a small taster from my flask, but felt one of my coughing fits coming upon me, so quickly pulled out a hanky, moving from my gardener's sight.

I opened the white cotton and there were several globules of blood. I recall if I am not mistaken that made it three such occurrences in the past 24 hours. I think before I continue this missive and the revelations from the good Albert I need to confess to the reader.

I omitted to tell, for no sinister reason, that on my last visit to London I did indeed meet with my specialist who informed me that the condition of my lungs had deteriorated, though indeed there was nothing to immediately worry about, but to expect an increase in coughing episodes.

He did assure me, much to my relief, there were many years left in me, but my breathing might at times be laboured along with an increase in blood splatters. In fact, I should expect to be quite uncomfortable at times as I became older.

Still, I digress, to continue with Albert's tale I was indeed again most intrigued.

'Well, sir, before I tells more of Miss Anna I need to bring in another character and this be Clifford. Now, his origins be a little patchy but suffice to say he was, so he said, from Bodmin Moor. His parents had perished so he was in effect an orphan, though we were not sure about any of his story. Now, he arrived late one afternoon in the winter at The Ship. There had been snow and the poor lad was almost near to collapse. He always professed to be aged 16, but in my estimate he was nearer to 13/14. Anyways, me and Ted warmed him up, gave him some brandy and then fed him. I tells thee, the way he ate I am sure it was his first meal in an age.'

He stopped to sup his tea and take a bite from some shortbread Nancy had kindly brought with her.

'Now then, oh yes, now Ted gave him the old groom's bed in the stable for the night and then we fetched Mrs Watson. She ran a reputable boarding house, mainly for transient fishermen, so her place be quite seasonal, but she took pity on the lad and offered to give him room and keep if he worked in lieu of payment until he could find proper employment. I can tell thee, good sir, it was an arrangement that benefited both parties, for he was a hard grafter and set about putting right the many repairs that were required on Mrs Watson's property. Then the winter went and the spring fishing season was upon us once more. He happened at the docks one morning when one of the many ships' captains was seeking help. He applied and was accepted.'

He again stopped for a quick slurp of tea, to which I readily refilled his cup and gained a smile and nod in thanks.

'Now, excusing the pun but he took to the sea like a fish out of water, so to speak, and quickly earned the confidence and respect of the skipper, who upped his wages and gave him more responsibility. Now, things went on the same for about three years, the boy growing into a handsome young man: all the girls thought he a marvel. He be tall, dark flowing hair and built like an ox, these piercing eyes – um, thems I remember, and had the most wonderful mannerism, always had time for everyone. Yes indeed, for a young lad a true gentle giant. Oh and I must not forget his devilish humour. Now, it was about another year hence and all seemed well. He settled into our village life quite amiably, but all's I can think being so young he had itchy feet and ambitions, he began drinking at The Sloop, a somewhat den of iniquity, down by the quay, and got in with a group who we all knew were smuggling, using their fishing boat as cover. Now thems would nip over to France and bring baccy, brandy, rum and suchlike – you know all very small fry but of course still illegal, not that we worried much. We's just grateful to get hold of the stuff at a price we could afford.'

He stopped for breath and I was grateful, for his speed of diction was rather quite fast.. Then he pulled out his pipe, carefully refilling the bowl, before lighting up and once again continued. I was indeed also drawn to this new character and wanted to hear more.

'Now then, one summer it was the annual fair at Penzance. All from miles around would attend: it was a much-loved yearly event. The Westlake family were in attendance, including the lovely Anna, who was rarely allowed out and kept very much under the watchful eye of her strict father.'

'However, today the sun was shining, music playing. All, rich and poor, were determined to have a good time. Though mostly a fair of country pursuits and local crafts, there was also the travelling variety with a helter-skelter, swings and the like.'

'Now, young Clifford was showing off his muscles on that ring-the-bell thingy, you knows where you have a mallet and tried to make it ring. Well, let me tell you he had quite a crowd of supporters and much to the annoyance of the stallholder made it ring several times, gaining a number of prizes before he was banned.'

'It was there that they first set eyes upon each other, a chance meeting with Anna who was giving admiring applause, whilst her father was off to the beer tent and her mother was looking at craft stalls. Inexplicably she had been allowed to wander off without a chaperone.'

'Now, Miss Anna had not made the acquaintance of many young men, only at stuffy balls and arranged meets with appropriate suitors, so young Clifford was quite an eye-opener. It is said they fell for each other that day but she being a lady kept him at arm's length.'

'Apparently he turned at her clapping, immediately taken with her beauty. "Why, thank you, Mistress, indeed very kind." She smiled and replied cheekily, "Bet you could not do it again, I counted five out of seven attempts: just a fluke, I would say."'

'"Well, now, Miss, I would like to prove you wrong but sadly I have been banned: too many prizes, see." He held aloft a number of cheap-looking items then selected a cuddly teddy bear. "Here, Miss, for you to remember the fair." She blushed, not quite knowing how to react but took the gift. "Now then, Miss?"

"Just Miss is enough for now."

"Very well, but I am Clifford at your service." He bowed. "Right, now fancy some fun? Hear that crashing? That's the smash-the-crockery stall. I bets thee I can win another prize."

"Mm, very full of yourself, aren't you?"

He smiled back, laughing. "Yes, I suppose I am. Come on, race you."

"Really, Master Clifford? And me in a dress and all no, I can't, I will follow."

"Well, then, as you is a true lady I will walk at your pace.'"

'They arrived at the crockery stall whereupon Clifford demolished a whole row, qualifying for a prize.'

"I can beat that, watch," she challenged.'

'And to everyone's astonishment she demolished the same amount but with two balls, not three. "See, helping your brother at cricket has some uses."'

Albert continued. 'Now apparently they laughed together until the bellowing voice of Mr Westlake was heard. He went into a fit of rage, screaming at the hapless young man, in fact whipping him with his riding crop. The lad backed off and ran into the crowd completely in shock and did not know what he had done wrong. Now, this was probably the worst action the master could have done as the continuing story will show.'

'Now the reason I have such first-hand knowledge is, as

I said earlier, I took her under my wing, so to speak. A big chance if Mr Westlake had found out, but I had seen her grow from a little girl and knew she was out of her depth and had no one to turn to for advice. I was indeed a father figure.'

'Indeed, I warned her off pursuing this man, explaining she was quite out of his league, but as I will show, sadly to no avail. They would try and meet as often as possible, which was hardly at all, in fact. I remember he actually sneaked into the grounds on a couple of occasions. She was smitten, I can tell you, and maybe a touch of forbidden fruit, I don't rightly know.'

'Now after the situation with the son and his death, Master Westlake became even more protective of Miss Anna, and mother Mistress Evelyn turned more and more to drink, though at this point it had not gotten out of control.'

'Oh please, sir, I should like to point out that I did not encourage young Anna when I say I helped her. I was in an awkward position. See, don't want you to think ill of me.'

'No, indeed, Albert. I am not thinking any the worse of you, but am greatly intrigued as to where you are going with this.'

He smiled, relighting his trusty old pipe. 'Wells, now, where was I? Oh yes, as I says, this liaison went on for a time. They would meet for a picnic or if Miss Anna rode out without a companion, then sometimes she would sneak down to the smugglers' cove from the house when it was low tide. They were very careful and no one but me knew of their meetings.'

'Now, this was a bleak time for the family, losing both the baby and then their son. Though the master had become more protective towards young Anna, she was still not a male, an heir, but having said that, he treated her as a princess, and perhaps a tad too protectively.'

'Once a week with her mother it was a trip to Truro and the department store to purchase the newest fashions, the latest books and the like. All seemed well but Miss Anna was falling more under Clifford's spell, and he for her.'

'Now, I am no expert but to me, they was deeply in love. Then about this time Mr Westlake began taking more trips to London to manage his business affairs and as the war progressed so the demand for his munitions increased, especially when there was a big push, the odd couple of days turning into a week.'

'Now, the mistress was really in a downward spiral and was drinking from morning to night, not caring about much else; even the trips to the city dwindled but of course this gave Miss Anna just the opportunity to visit her man.'

'Now, Clifford was doing good by himself: the smuggling business had brought him in a tidy sum, I can tell thee. He dressed in finer clothes and even had his own rented cottage on the edge of the village, perfect for illicit meetings, not that I am saying anything bad about Miss Anna's character.'

I grinned to myself: this must be hard for the man to recite, but I had a great deal of sympathy and was not judgemental. I just wanted him to get to the point. Now also at this juncture I have made the decision to cut out some of his story, as a number of the facts are irrelevant, and strangely I again felt tangs of jealousy, completely bizarre.

'……..So, Captain, their relationship continued and they became slightly careless. There were a few tongues wagging.

I did warn her, but, as they say, love can be blind. Now when young Clifford was out on his fishing/smuggling trips he could be gone for a day or sometimes more. I knows they had to be extra-careful in France because of the war. So anyhow, when he was away Miss Anna would keep watch from the battlements for sight of the returning boat, and as I recall he used to raise a flag to indicate their return. Wells, she would dance like there was no tomorrow round and round, the happiest person alive.'

I pondered to myself. Now it was falling into place. On the occasions I had seen Anna she was either looking pensively out to the ocean or dancing: it suddenly became clear.

'Now I remember this day well, it was a Thursday. Mistress Evelyn was out cold from the drink and Mr Westlake was in London attending his business, but on this occasion he returned two days early unannounced. Clifford had also just come back from a successful trip laden with booty, so he had a reserve of cash which he wanted to lavish on Anna. They had travelled separately to Penzance and had met at a small restaurant near to the harbour front, it was a place where lovers would meet, dimly lit little alcoves and candles. It was here he proposed marriage, which she accepted without a thought.'

'I recollect her telling me at some point, but before I must continue with a circumstance which could not be planned and a coincidence that happened to ruin the girl's life.'

'They had been supping champagne and were making their way back to the cab rank near to the station when Mr Westlake alighted from the London train. He was also making his way to the taxis, but on seeing the pair together flew into another blind rage, raining blows onto the young man. To his credit, Clifford could have easily retaliated, choosing instead to take the punishment. As folks have later said, the lad was left in the gutter, a mass of bruises and blood, and the master had to drag his daughter, screaming and objecting. During the return journey to the hall, slightly tipsy, she told him they were betrothed, at which he went into another rage, locking her in her rooms and forbidding her from leaving Morgwel without a chaperone.'

Albert excused himself for the toilet and I remember reflecting on his prose of the past couple of hours that was now sounding, as he progressed, more and more like a novel. I also took the opportunity for a quick snifter.

'Sorry about that, Captain, sir.'

'That's fine, pray continue.'

The evening was beginning to draw in so I offered Albert a drop of malt, which he readily accepted, enquiring if in lieu of the fact he had not tended the gardens much, would I require him the next day, to which I agreed.

'So, sir, the next I find somewhat disturbing. Mr Westlake employed a lady chaperone and a male bodyguard to be with Miss Anna at all times. She was not allowed from the property and was in effect a prisoner. Mistress Evelyn voiced her feeble objections but was more interested in the drink and could easily be pacified.'

'So things bubbled along. Miss Anna was allowed back onto the battlements and could often see her betrothed from afar. He still raised the flag on his return and she danced her jig.

Now what's I about to tell thee is somewhat sinister and some mere conjecture, but the outcome is just as sad.'

He paused, taking a large amount of malt which I readily topped back up.

'So, though the master allowed Miss Anna to the battlements he was still displeased with her liaison with this young man, whom I believed he even tried to buy off but to no avail. So this one day Clifford set sail for France but on this occasion the ship had not returned for over a week. I tell thee she was beside herself, pacing the castle worried beyond, then came the news. The ship had run aground off the French coast. Though all had survived they to a man had been captured by the Army and put in prison. As the story goes, Clifford was shot dead whilst trying to escape. Now young Anna was inconsolable: she wept, refused food and continued to look out from the castle.'

'Now there was a rumour at the time that Master Westlake had paid off the other members of the boat and that it was all a set-up, but that is another fact that we will probably never know. Now Miss Anna became more distraught, then one day the boat returned: the crew and captain had managed to secure a French yard to repair the minor damage, but of course there was no Clifford. The men were all cagey but corroborated the story that Clifford had been shot dead.'

Albert paused, composing himself. 'Then here's is, well, the sad part. A week after the return of the boat, having kept a vigil in hope, there had been a mistake. Anna threw herself from the grounds of the hall to the sea below. Her body was never found, more than likely swept away with the tides to who knows where. But the tragedy is that a few days later Clifford returned alive and well: on this occasion he had escaped and somehow managed to find his way back to England, then Cornwall. Well, he was beside himself with grief on hearing Anna's death. He simply packed his bags and left and to this day no one has ever heard from him.'

'Now, Mr Westlake was a different matter: he could not accept her death and spent all his time on the battlements scouring the sea for her body with powerful binoculars. He would sit for hours clutching pictures of Anna distraught and grieving beyond, blaming himself for her death, then he would walk along the shoreline in search of her body. See, that's the puzzle. Sadly, it was I who saw her jump: it was from the clifftop at Morgwel and I knows it's not a sheer drop. You see, the rocks stick out somewhat so she would have hit them on her fall and probably be dead before she hit the sea. Now I knows what I saw: she threw herself willingly. Such a tragedy, someone so young with their whole life ahead.'

'So eventually he accepted the awful reality and the Westlakes went into mourning for the third time. It was then that they left the hall for London never to return, and the rest you know. The place remained empty until we have the good fortune of you, dear Captain, becoming the new owner.'

I was quite taken aback and moved by the story and it left me quite emotionally drained. Of course the intriguing part was that Anna's body had not been found. I thanked Albert profusely for his rendition and selected a bottle of malt as a thankyou. I cannot say how pleased this made him.

CHAPTER 16

Now I settled to ponder on the history. Having poured a large glass of whisky I lit a Player's then sat beside the fire in the second living room adjacent to the entrance to the castle. My mind was whirring: so much to take in but what a tragic ending, I concluded.

Then I was inexplicably drawn to the old ruin. I have no explanation but just knew I needed to be at the battlements. I remember I positively bounded up the stairs before reaching the top and there she was, the beautiful Anna standing quite still, looking not at the sea or dancing, but straight towards myself.

Her face lit up. She was glowing, her beauty beyond anything I had ever beheld. The smile was so captivating, but of course I was still puzzled. I walked towards her and this time she did not move or disappear. Her body was now not translucent; in fact, I felt I could touch her. Then she held her hand up, beckoning me to stop, then indicated she wanted me to follow.

She walked past me, and in doing so caused a slight movement of air which was still cold, almost icy. Then I caught a whiff of what I can only assume was perfume; I savoured this moment. She approached the stairs, beckoning me to follow, but there was still something odd: it was as if she were, well, floating, her feet not quite touching the stones.

Several mysteries were solved but the one in front of me was unfathomable. I followed her, thinking, 'I would pursue her to the ends of the earth.' I recall asking her to speak; there was no sound but a definite reaction, and she smiled again, drawing me further in.

That evening we sat in the living room. No words were exchanged but she was in my presence for at least 45 minutes before she once more disappeared: that night I was the happiest man alive. I retired to my rooms, her image firmly emblazoned in my subconscious.

Now I will say that I had become almost a recluse, for over the next few days I would not venture far in the hope I would have a liaison with Anna. I cut Nancy's hours short so that I could be alone each evening when she seemed to manifest more often.

As each time we were together passed, so she became clearer to me, though still no words, until one night – though I must confess to having consumed an enormous amount of malt – she spoke clearly.

'Captain, sir, my love, our love transcends even death. I wish to be with you forever. You know what you must do.'

Then she again disappeared. I was somewhat perplexed, as I must confess I did not know what to do. Madam Rose had said the same so for now I had to content myself with the occasional company of Anna.

Things carried on much the same for several days until suddenly one evening I realised what was needed of me, and

to follow my destiny I would need much braveness for I knew
I had to be with Anna forever.

CHAPTER 17

Truro Coroner's Court, September 1921.

The Coroner looked up from his papers and surveyed the room. Clearing his throat, he proceeded. 'So we have before us a death that saddens me deeply. Captain Andrew Williamson, a young man in the prime of life taken before time, so we are gathered here today to try and ascertain what happened. I have letters that will tell of his state of mind, statements and eyewitnesses.'

Albert and Nancy were the last to see the captain alive and were called to testify.

'The final time I saw the captain he was smiling, in fact laughing, then he leapt from the clifftop. I was shocked at his actions for not long before he had told me he now knew his true destiny then, then, well, this….' He bowed his head.

Nancy gave her statement, then there was a report from a Professor Richardson, who had helped Williamson back to good health. He described the captain as cured but possibly still somewhat mentally unstable at times, but was adamant that in his opinion the captain would not have taken his own life.

The proceedings continued with a result of death by misadventure. There was no suicide note, in fact the last thing he had written was, 'Love transcends even death', left in the kitchen under a bottle of malt, which of course to all was a mystery. So that is the end of the tale and Morgwel went up for sale.

Six months later.

Estate agent Mr James slowed the car to a halt outside Morgwel: it was the first viewing since the hall had come back to market following the captain's demise. In the back were the Smythe family: Mum, Dad and their 12-year-old son.

'My, a magnificent property,' observed Mr Smythe, 'and goodness me, just look at those battlements.' He turned to his son. 'Hey, Bill, you will have a great deal on fun there, eh, old boy?' He smiled in return, anxious to explore what could be his new domain.

Williamson's solicitor, who had control of the estate, was waiting in the drive to greet the party.

James guided the family towards the front door, but young Bill stood back, admiring the castle ruins, then shouted, 'Excuse me, sir, but who is that in the battlements? There is a woman dancing and a soldier in uniform waving a stick and smiling.'

They all turned and gazed up but naturally there was no one to be seen apart from the solicitor Stevens who lingered. He immediately recognised his old friend, the captain. He smiled to himself, waved at the battlements, then continued about his business but not before Williamson and Anna waved back.

On that day they disappeared, never to be seen again, apart from by Albert, the ageing gardener who would often spy them on the battlements. Though they never acknowledged him, she was always dancing and he smiling. He kept his secret to the grave.

EPILOGUE

For all you animal-lovers I thought it prudent to explain the fate of Dougy, the dog, and Willy, the cat. I trust you enjoyed my humour naming them after WWI figures, or rather the captain's.

Following the tragedy, gardener Albert befriended both animals. He had previously been contacted by the solicitor Stevens who gave him instructions to look after the hall and continue tending the gardens whilst he tied up all the legalities.

Albert agreed to stay at Morgwel, to render his duties more easily, and also for security purposes. Now Willy spent his days, as cats do, exploring the hall and grounds, though often ventured to the battlements where his demeanour would change.

Dougy, however, would not settle, ignored his food and spent the days searching for his lost master. He pined, often wailing, on occasion climbing to the battlements where he would curl up close to the thorn bush where Williamson had often spent his time.

One morning Albert found him curled up on the captain's bed quite dead and duly buried him in the grounds.

Willy continued to live there and was adopted by the new

owners. He still visited the battlements and old Albert would swear he often heard the scraping of Dougy's paws on the stone floor.

The captain and Anna were seen again, on the odd occasion and only by Albert. They would be looking out to sea arm-in-arm, happy and content. She would sometimes even dance but as the years passed their sightings became less and less.

The End